Listen to the Trees

Patti Sapp

The front cover image is an original painting created by Patti Sapp.

Patti Sapp is the Managing Director and Practitioner at Quiet Time Hypnosis, LLC. She can be reached at www.qthypnosis.com

First Edition: August, 2020 Printed in the USA.

ISBN 978-1-7354768-2-7

Contents

Willie

"Who names a tree?" Amanda's oldest friend, Catherine, complained through the phone's receiver. "It's plain silly."

Amanda listened compassionately, knowing Catherine had no imagination. She was used to her friend's rejections when it came to interesting endeavors. Amanda expected such logic from someone who had lived her entire life in a vanilla sort of way. Plain vanilla ice cream, in the safety of a Styrofoam bowl. Not even in a cone. Eaten carefully with a white plastic spoon, avoiding any possibility of messy drips. That summed up her oldest and dearest friend perfectly.

Amanda lived her life in a banana split manner. With extra cherries, sticky, syrupy nuts and gobs of gooey chocolate. And why not include piles of whipped cream and colorful sprinkles for the hell of it? She was creative, a spontaneous visionary, and often unconventional. She was sometimes viewed as peculiar. Some would go as far to say that Amanda was out of touch with reality. Did she care? "What people think of me is none of my business." Amanda believed the words of wisdom she once read on a tea bag.

Catherine had always followed the rules. During those older teen and early twenty-something days, she watched in horror when some of their friends, including Amanda, had gone skinny dipping in the farmer's pond. She always disappeared when they passed the bong around at parties. As young adults, Amanda invited Catherine to join her on traveling adventures, with high hopes to learn about other cultures. Catherine never accepted the invitations. She consistently made excuses.

Catherine and Amanda had remained friends, despite their obvious differences. Amanda pitied those who lived in a small, protected manner. She understood that lifestyle decisions are always a choice. Catherine was predictable, which made the relationship easy. She was also kind and sensitive. Amanda cherished the friendship she had with Catherine.

Over the years, Amanda had slept in hostels, sampled foods from around the world, and enjoyed other cultures through wonderful and risky experiences. Catherine was content to stay home. Amanda had lived a colorful and adventurous life, with few regrets. Most of her adventures had become outrageous party stories, often a bit exaggerated.

There was one unsavory situation that remained in her memory, never to be shared... that incident in the Amazon. They called the musky concoction a brew, made of a variety of plants. "Oh, if it's anything like highly caffeinated coffee, I'm going to love this," was her initial thought. The elders of the tribe didn't share much information, but she'd trekked all the way through the dense jungle in the sweltering humidity. She was certain that creating a truly authentic experience was the best approach in these situations. "This is going to be awesome. Can't wait to experience this mystery!"

My, that brew they called Ayahuasca resulted in an out-of-body, altered state of consciousness she wouldn't choose to repeat, ever. There were brief moments of sheer ecstasy. "It's like I'm in a wet painting, and the colors are swirling and dripping all over me. I'm swimming in a rainbow. This is so cool!"

She also recalled not knowing if she was standing up or lying down. "Where are my legs? I can't feel my body!" The confusion was horrifying. Bloody scratches on her thighs later were reminders of her attempts to feel the numb appendages with her fingernails. Unbelievable. She might have been singing, as well as dancing. Maybe she heard someone else singing? Was there music, or was she dancing to the beat of her own internal drum? Some of the experience remained a total mystery, not a fun type of mystery though. It was unsettling. Thank goodness she didn't know any of the other participants and was across the globe at the time. It's not like she was going to run into any of them at Happy Hour or in a yoga class now, right?

Oh my, the amazing euphoria, followed by an unbelievable crash. "I feel like I've been slammed into the side of a brick building. My head is pounding. And my brain is lost in a fog of brown and gray." She honestly wouldn't wish that crash on anyone. It also included the nauseating fact that every single meal she had eaten that week was left on the rainforest floor. So embarrassing.

She decided long ago to let it go as a stupid mistake.

Let's just say that was a regret she did not care to discuss.

Years later, when simply viewing a photo of a Cinchona tree, Amanda experienced an uncontrollable wave of nausea. She discovered later the tree is well-known globally as the source of quinine, an important medication used to treat malaria. Unfortunately, it was also a harsh reminder of that horrible rainforest mistake for Amanda. Decades had passed since the Ayahuasca decision. Amanda now viewed the incident as a severe learning experience. "If only I could go back in time, have a do-over. I'd erase the plant-based brew, which turned out to be nothing like coffee. I'd even be willing to delete the cool parts," she reminisced.

After the "It's just plain silly to name a tree!" phone conversation with her best friend had ended, Amanda went out to visit Willie, her favorite tree. She hadn't even told Willie about the Amazon fiasco; some life choices were not meant to be repeated or shared. As a mature woman now, she was thankful for this fascinating relationship that involved nothing that ever needed to be deleted.

Today she rested beneath the familiar and friendly oak, with a heavy heart.

Ninety-eight days and counting since the shelter in place had begun.

There didn't seem to be an end in sight. Millions had succumbed to the virus around the globe, as had thousands in her community. She was home safe, but lonely and deeply saddened by the enormity of deaths and suffering she heard about each day. Like Catherine, and everyone else, she was currently home for an unforeseen amount of time. Her cottage was a wonderful place to be stuck. If only she could relax and enjoy it like a vacation from the noisy world instead of feeling caged and confined.

The pandemic had made so many fearful, including Amanda. Other than her four legged Dalilah Belle, Amanda lived alone.

"What if I were to get sick? Who would care for me?" she wondered aloud with no one to respond.

She took her temperature multiple times a

day, just because. Dr Ni, her acupuncturist had suggested a variety of herbs, meant to combat anxiety. She hadn't been consistent about taking them. "The herbs will only help you if take them." Dr Ni reminded her with kindness at each visit.

Usually she followed her acupuncture's advice and received wonderful results from the strange herbs and concoctions he recommended. She liked to think of him more as a medicine man or shaman than a physician. She trusted him. He was highly trained and would never give her any type of plant-based craziness she used in her younger days when in the Amazon rainforest. She loved the fact there were no lab coats or formalities during her visits with Dr. Ni. His uniform consisted of worn jeans and whatever he grabbed from his closet. Hawaiian shirts, flannel, or chambray, depending on the day.

Their discussions included favorite flavors of Ben & Jerry's ice cream and the most efficient ways to bundle sage for smudging. She taught him to include dried lavender or bay leaves in his sage bundles for an extra dose of serenity. Amanda often wondered if Dr. Ni was married, or if was seeing anyone. He was a fascinating and intelligent man. She always looked forward to visits and wished they'd last longer. She wondered if he thought of her as a knowledgable and interesting patient or just a wacky old lady?

"Is this a secret crush?" she chuckled at herself and dismissed the ridiculous thought.

She'd never forget the visit when Dr. Ni took her on an impromptu, personal tour of his greenhouse. Growing in the corner, along with his sage and other familiar herbs, were several large cannabis plants. She still called it weed or pot, but now that it had become legal, the plant apparently required a more proper name. She was fully aware cannabis wasn't one of the naturopathic options he offered his patients, that he grew the plant for his own personal use. She liked this man even more now. She imagined he consumed it with great care. The leafy plant was probably organically grown and selected for the strain's specific benefits. She felt as if they shared a secret. A little thrill on an average day for a nutty old lady.

Fitful dreams and worries had dominated her nights for weeks. She had no one to confide her insecurities. Plus, she was known as fearless, the risk taker. This vulnerable feeling was unfamiliar, and she wasn't sure she wanted to admit it to anyone. This whole vulnerable thing was uncharacteristic and confusing.

She wished she had some of that cannabis in Dr. Ni's greenhouse to calm her down. She'd given up weed a few decades earlier, but maybe it was time to pay him another visit? She considered confiding in Catherine, who would surely understand fear. It appeared she lived her entire life sheltered because of it. Unfortunately, sharing personal feelings with Catherine usually did not end well. Amanda would have loved to open up and talk to Catherine; she knew her insights could be helpful. Catherine just wasn't comfortable hearing or even talking about emotions.

Amanda understood she was one of the fortunate ones. She had her own spacious yard to move and tinker in the sunshine. The garden was thriving, and she enjoyed a view of farmland behind her home along with a nearby forest that always brought forth flurries of squirrel activities. Even during a pandemic, the squirrels just kept living their best life, carefree. Amanda shared Willie, the oak tree in her back yard, with all the creatures: her favorite owls, the wood thrush with beautiful songs, one gorgeous and distinctive cardinal, a velvety blue bird.

Situated near healthy mounds of French lavender, Amanda inhaled the fragrance as she anticipated another connection with this ancient oak tree. It was most certainly a unique friendship. She had a connection with the tree she hadn't found with others. Maybe it was twin flame thing, or a past life memory. She didn't need to understand what they shared to experience the intimate connection. It felt like Willie could hear and respond to her thoughts. The connection could only be described as magical. Even Dalilah Belle, her sweet dog, seemed to intentionally disappear during her curious meditative times with the oak tree in their backyard to give them privacy.

The tree was solid and dependable as she leaned her petite body into his welcoming trunk.

She lovingly nicknamed the oak, Willie, after the popular songwriter - a simple man, perhaps underappreciated for his depth of knowledge. Much like this backyard friend, her oak tree was willing to share wisdom. Willie's tales enveloped her mind like vivid dreams with each special encounter. Amanda snuggled next to Willie, leaning her head against his trunk, her long silver strands tickled his deeply carved bark.

Anticipating Willie's message, Amanda began her ritual of rhythmic breath-work from low in her belly. She started with a single deep breath in through her nose, smelling the fragrant blossoms nearby. She released the air through her lips as if blowing out one of her homemade candles. She repeated this familiar practice until she fell into the kind of hypnotic trance that allowed communication to begin.

A familiar calmness wound through her body like a caress of a gentle breeze. The soft ground beneath her supported her petite body as she was transported to a world of messages and lessons that Willie created for her.

If this were the first time that she'd experienced the old oak's powers, she'd be shocked. "Out of touch with reality" was what people said about her jokingly. If only they knew! As a long-time companion, however, Willie had taken her on so many adventures, nothing seemed to surprise her anymore.

As she began to quiet her mind and body,

Amanda then used a simple progressive muscle relaxation technique. She imagined an orb of calming light above the crown of her head. It was about the size of a grapefruit. As Amanda visualized this orb of peaceful energy, it began to melt down across her shoulders. Such calmness. Her arms, torso and down to her fingertips were softening and easily participating. Eventually the tranquility extended down through the lower portion of her body. Exquisite deep comfort and incredible relaxation allowed Willie's story to unfold, Amanda an entranced observer.

□□□□□□□□□□□□□□□□□□□

Amanda saw a young and lively Forest Sage with a crown of tiny white flowers atop her voluminous curls, which were the hues of the brightest carnelian imaginable. She was known as a wise beauty with natural powers of healing among those residing in the oak grove. She danced and swayed to the music of the wind, moving her ample hips with uninhibited joy.

Celtic songs of old sounded through the breeze and summoned bluebirds from miles away. The bluebirds circled and peered down as she bent to examine the clover beneath her bare feet. She held a hand-woven basket filled with a variety of herbs and treasures found on the floor of the oak grove.

Locating a valuable four-leaf clover was her passion in that moment. They were hidden inconspicuously among patches of other less interesting clover and green plants. As a member of the druids, the Forest Sage knew how the clover, also called shamrocks, brought good fortune and luck. The chances of finding these treasures in the wild were one in ten thousand, yet this young Forest Sage, sent by Willie, seemed to know exactly where to look. Her confident ivory feet led her in a magical sort of way directly to the most perfect shamrock.

The Forest Sage smiled a secret smile as she thought of the lucky woman called Amanda. She was given the task of locating the most beautiful of all four-leafed clovers to leave as an important message.

The message was on her heart, despite the fact that she'd never have an opportunity to meet the silver-haired lady that Willie fancied so much.

The note, carved on a delicate oak slat, was one of good fortune and health. It was to be left with the most perfect four-leaf clover for Amanda to discover when the trance had come to an end. The Forest Sage followed the directions given to her with care and precision. Entrusted with this task was an honor, not to be taken lightly in the grove of oaks.

□□□□□□□□□□□□□□□□□□□

Amanda woke from the trance dizzy and confused, as if she'd been in a deep sleep for a very long time. During these meditative times with Willie, time had no meaning. She noticed darkness had set in.

She gazed up at the waxing crescent moon. A beautiful night for star gazing. If she hadn't been disoriented from Willie's experience, she would have taken more time to enjoy it. As she stretched to regain her footing, she moved towards the backdoor of her cottage. Bending down as she passed near her herb garden, she plucked a few mint leaves to settle her anxious stomach. Her foot hit the wooden slat on the ground. She picked it up and noticed an attached organza bag tied with twine. Entering the kitchen, she eagerly turned on the light to see the treasure Willie had left for her:

"Allow fear to fly away with the wind."

The poignant carved message lifted a weight from her slender shoulders that she had not been aware of. She released a long sigh. Had she been holding her breath? She wasn't sure. She felt light and relieved as she untied the twine and opened the bag to find the most magnificent emerald green four-leaf clover she'd ever seen.

She placed the treasures lovingly with the others, a whole collection, on her fireplace mantle.

Lying her head on the feather pillow felt like a gift as she anticipated a restorative sleep. Her long silver hair feathered out, circling her head like a crown. She thought of the Forest Sage with the tiny white flowers in her glowing hair as she drifted off the sleep. The bedroom window was left open so when the sun arose, her first view would be Willie.

The slight breeze entered her room, touching her skin with a divine purpose. The breezes became more noticeable, yet Amanda slept soundly. She was vaguely aware of the wind delicately rustling her cotton nightgown throughout the night, blowing away and clearing out worries. She awoke, fears released, well rested and joyful.

A Song

Amanda wandered through her yard checking on flowers and vegetables. She was enjoying her newfound energy this morning, not focused on any particular task. Her steps were lively and child-like as she passed by the cedar planter filled with strawberries, almost ready to be harvested. The berries would accompany the Cannoli Ben & Jerry's ice cream for a delicious dessert sometime soon.

Her mind drifted to her beloved Oliver. Amanda had been married to Oliver for more than half of her life. He had built that strawberry planter. Not surprisingly, the structure still stood in one piece and was fully functional. Just like Oliver himself, his work was sturdy and always helpful.

Amanda gazed across the yard at the hand carved bench and matching picnic table near the vegetables. How many glasses of tea had they consumed, and how many conversations had taken place sitting on that bench?

Oliver's handiwork was evident in almost every corner of her world. That was how he demonstrated his love all of those years ago. He built, created, and shared his talents in his own silent manner.

"Oh, Ollie, how I miss our times together," she whispered to the birds nearby. He used to poke fun at her for talking to the birds, she recalled fondly.

"Not much has changed, has it?" she said, as the birds flew overhead paying no attention to the odd, child-like lady murmuring aloud to no one. A distinctive bluebird peaked down at her from its perch on a lower branch with a curious look that made her chuckle.

Oliver had been her first and only lover. Together for several decades, it had not occurred to her that she'd be living out her final years without him. The hand carved mantle in the living room was also his handiwork. During the winter months she kept a fire lit throughout most days, sometimes dreaming of Oliver's warmth.

As thoughts of the winter fires drifted through her mind, Amanda realized the sun was shining. She lifted her chin to the sky to let the warm glow touch her cheeks. She smiled and sighed with pleasure. She loved the sunshine.

She gathered sticks from the yard, knowing they would be helpful to start fires when the weather turned cold. Always prepared, she kept an antique copper tub filled with kindling. Willie had provided enough kindling for countless fires as she added to the growing pile.

Amanda cherished the time spent in her back yard. Inside her cottage, although quaint and cozy, was cluttered. Closets filled with a lifetime of living. Drawers and cabinets stuffed with outdated papers and receipts. Oliver's clothing still hung in his half of the closet, untouched. She retreated to her back yard for the open spaces and fresh air.

Gathering sticks for the warm fire was a way to keep herself busy and productive, and made it easy to ignore the overwhelming mess. Oliver had not been a tidy man, and to be honest, she was not much better.

Creativity had been cherished and honored in their home. Creative minds are rarely neat. They had once walked into a bookstore and the shelves were white and spotless. Books were arranged meticulously. The floors gleamed, and the lights were florescent. Within seconds, their eyes met, automatically heading for the exit without a word. Their favorite literary destination was a delightful mess of mysteries. The floor was covered with mismatched wool carpets and there were nooks and crannies stuffed with interesting books. Worn chairs and crooked stools were scattered throughout the rooms. The best literary finds were hidden and required ninja moves, possibly a high-powered flashlight, and ingenuity.

"Is it even a bookstore if there are no shenanigans involved?" Oliver and Amanda had often joked with one another; neither of them enjoyed boring and over-organized stores. They preferred shopping to be an adventure, like a treasure hunt.

That delightful bookstore destination was almost a replica of their cottage, a place where magical thoughts and splendor happened. The dust bunnies had names. Oliver and Amanda were perfectly content.

Willie's message from the previous evening had a lasting impact, Amanda realized. The fear she'd been experiencing had disappeared. Her day was peaceful and free from worries. The powers of that tree were incredible. More aware of her surroundings now, she was able to appreciate her life. It was time, finally, to attack the challenge of cleaning her cottage. The procrastination, the grief or maybe laziness had given her reasons to spend time outdoors. She promised herself the time had come.

The kitchen was always a good place to start her organizing, since she spent so much time there. As she considered this task, she remembered she was due to visit the market today to replenish supplies.

The nearby farmer's market was so close, she could walk. Just a few weeks ago she had purchased enough greens and vegetables to last for quite a while. The fresh raspberries were tasty morning treats and she made jam with the leftovers. They even had a variety of delicious cheeses for sale, which was one of her favorite indulgences. Amanda felt healthy carrying the basket of colorful, fresh fruits and vegetables home, like a proud child with a trophy. Little did her neighbors know that in addition to her rainbow of veggies, she also had a ridiculous amount of chocolate and ice cream in her kitchen.

"Of course, ice cream is a food group!" she frequently told herself. "It's called balance."

A quick trip to the farmer's market gave Amanda a bit of exercise and allowed her to procrastinate about cleaning. She noticed that her steps were lively. She was back home in record time. She had found plenty for herself at the market today, and even the kind of handcrafted peanut butter dog treats Dalilah Belle liked. She offered a little chunk of the peanut butter treat from her pocket and the dog gobbled it up. Her fluffy tail made it clear she was pleased. If she could express herself verbally, Amanda would have heard a resounding, "Thanks, Mom!" with a generous amount of saliva dripping from her face. Amanda popped a dark chocolate square with a touch of sea salt in her mouth and let it melt on her tongue. Her gentle and funny dog, Dalilah Belle was her constant, if not sometimes annoying companion. They liked their balanced life together.

"It's a decent life," she reminded herself. "Better than decent. Extraordinary," she corrected her mindset.

Back in her yard, Amanda saw a bluebird

swoop down and play in her birdbath. Energetic yellow finches were having a gourmet meal at her feeder. The stargazer lilies were in full bloom, along with the mountain laurel bushes. The little delights had gone unnoticed far too long. Life had been moving forward, and she would follow the example of her friends in nature. "Yes, life is extraordinary!" she declared to herself and to the creatures who frequented her yard.

Moving towards the tree now, she decided it was time for some motivation and wisdom. She sat crossed legged on the bed of dried leaves. Her well-worn overalls were soft and comfortable. She leaned her silver-haired head against the oak and initiated her routine. Deep breathing. Eyes closed gently. Softness flowed through her cheeks, her shoulders and through her torso. As she relaxed, she melted her frame into the strong tree trunk.

Bill Withers, a singer she admired, and his song "Lean on Me" played in her mind for a few minutes until the hypnotic trance grew deeper. She was in a different place for this experience, created just for her by Willie. Music was included, but not of Bill Withers, or any other man.

□□□□□□□□□□□□□□□□□

She recognized the faint smell of the salty air immediately. It was reminiscent of the South Pacific, a place she had visited several times and loved.

Willie led her down a long, narrow walkway to a small wooden boat. Brilliant blue skies, lanky palm trees, azure water and salty breezes enveloped her senses. Sitting on a padded bench on the boat, she felt the gentle rocking motion of the water beneath her. It lulled her into a deeper state of bliss. Relaxed and tranquil, she succumbed to the rocking motion like a carefree infant drifting into a nap in the safe arms of a nurturing parent. Had minutes passed or hours? It didn't matter. Time didn't exist in Willie's tales.

Amanda heard the melodic songs of a whale. She heard the cries of birds overhead. She drifted further into this tropical paradise through Willie's safe guidance. She saw the color of blue that can only be associated with the depth of the ocean. She was there, gracefully swimming in the presence of this magnificent creature. Gliding through the water taking in the beauty of her surroundings she felt the vibrations of the whale's songs. Did they contain profound knowledge or secrets?

Amanda experienced a connection with this huge, gentle creature. She swam, floating and feeling the song of the whale move through her body as if she belonged there, a surprise gift from the sea. There was no other place on the entire planet she longed to be, connected to the song of this whale is where she was destined to be at this exact moment. So incredible.

Just floating, letting the water carry her. There was no destination, only calmness and peace.

The song became a story of hope for her. Without any words, she felt serenity caress her skin. The vibration of the whale's song touched the water and became the water. The lingering sensations became a part of her own heartbeat. The music was a part of her now, as if the whale knew she was there and was singing a song for just her. A personalized melody of peace.

Her body was gliding through the songs of the glorious animal. What a profound honor it was to be emerged in this melodic water. It felt like a magical dream. Still floating with no perception of time, she appreciated and attempted to memorize every moment.

□□□□□□□□□□□□□□□□□□□□

When she felt the sun on her face, she realized she was no longer immersed in the sea water. When she opened her eyes, Amanda expected to be on a boat, but what she saw was her own familiar yard. Sitting on the dried oak leaves, she touched her skin to see if there was moisture from the sea. Her hands and body were soft and dry. Her fingertips didn't lie, yet the episode seemed so incredibly real. As she sat in a daze, Dalilah Belle approached with something in her mouth. It was a small piece of driftwood.

Engraved in the well-worn, pale wood:

"When did you stop singing?"

Let it Be

On the third day of a rainy spell, Amanda was happily baking. Rain fell outside, mesmerizing and soothing. She didn't mind the rain, as a matter of fact it was pleasant inside of her cottage kitchen where she gazed at the rain through the window.

Amanda had done some brief organizing, now baking was her distraction. The small house was currently filled with the delectable aromas of cinnamon, clove, and nutmeg. She added the twist of extra spices to her rolls. She hoped to find neighbors to share with, realizing she was getting carried away with such abundance.

"Maybe Catherine would appreciate some," she thought. They hadn't communicated during the pandemic as often as she would have liked. Even though they were great friends, they weren't on the same wavelength these days. Catherine was busy with twin granddaughters. "Those angelic, and sometimes sassy girls are the reason I get up each morning," Catherine had confided to Amanda. It was rare that Catherine shared emotions. Amanda was delighted that her best friend demonstrated such passion, despite the fact she also felt slightly abandoned.

Her beloved Oliver would be openly sneaking cinnamon roll samples by now. The aromas were impossible to miss in the small home they shared. He'd compliment her and then teasingly blame her for his expanding waistline.

"When I was single, I was skinny; I'd rather be plump and content," he'd admit to her with a long, luxurious embrace. "You don't need Catherine's attention anyway, you have me."

She had briefly tuned into the news for world updates, but decided music was a much better choice. She turned the radio to an oldies station, and to her delight, the music was uplifting, despite the grayness outside her kitchen window. How on Earth did she manage to remember the words to so many songs from her youth?

Using the wooden mixing spoon as a microphone, she allowed the music to lead her into a lively mood.

Van Morrison had released "Brown Eyed Girl" in the sixties. Amanda found it funny that even her young neighbor, Casey, knew the words. Casey was a cute, redheaded teenager. When visiting, they had sung the song together once. It was a memory that came up almost every time she heard the song. Now she sang easily from memory and even twanged out the guitar chords, wishing Casey, who was now in her late twenties, was there to join in the fun.

Singing, swaying, and dancing around the kitchen on a rainy day felt good. When "Let it Be" by the Beatles came on, she sang every single word. Her voice and the well-known lyrics were both voices of wisdom and advocacy for a healthier, more loving planet. Simple songs. Memories of when life felt easy.

That's how her beloved Oliver had been. Easy. A man of few words.

We could go on a road trip and not say anything for hours, she recalled. Comfort in silence is a sign of a remarkable relationship, she thought, remembering a trip through the Smoky Mountains when they spent evenings around a dancing fire, wrapped in blankets. Blissful. Uncomplicated.

Dalilah Belle started barking at something through the window, the silence broken abruptly. The mail truck, the same one that arrived daily, yet her companion felt the need to loudly announce the arrival. Dalilah Belle wagged and pranced as if the visit was for just her.

The man in his blue polyester uniform, known in the neighborhood as Pete, approached her door with a brown cardboard box. Amanda handed Pete a generously filled plate with warm rolls. He took a long whiff and grinned. As far as Amanda knew, Pete was a bachelor. She imagined him sitting in front of the television with a frozen dinner or take-out after each long day. They shared their love for sweets, but she didn't know much else about Pete. He was the one that first introduced her to the Ben & Jerry's flavor, Cinnamon Bun. The ice cream featured caramel, a generous amount of spices and other yumminess swirled into a pint of heaven. She knew he'd enjoy her rolls, which were packed full of cinnamon.

She accepted the wet box from Pete with anticipation. She carefully balanced the cardboard box along with her dripping umbrella, which was embellished with rainbows. He gave Dalilah Belle a brief pat on the head, departing with his plate of spicy goodness and a congenial wave.

Sitting on the front porch now, out of the rain in a wooden rocking chair she held the package on her lap. This must be my art supplies, she thought happily as she tore into the box. Paints, brushes, blank canvases, ready for her masterpieces. What fun!

A few weeks back, she had discovered a worn easel in the attic. Dusting it off, she had grandiose ideas of painting beautiful castles perched on green grassy hills, soothing, flowing sapphire rivers and gorgeous gardens. She would paint with the most vibrant colors and display them on her mantle with her other treasures. Optimistic plans.

As she stood, contemplating the paints and brushes, her thoughts turned skeptical, which was uncharacteristic for Amanda. She immediately gave herself a pep talk as she carried the box into the house, placing it over behind the couch to deal with later. "I've always been creative. I can paint beautiful works of art. This is a totally reasonable idea." Amanda decided.

"I must remember that creativity can be used for the sheer fun of it and nothing more. My works of art don't have to be museum quality. "

Back in the kitchen, the reality of the therapeutic baking hit Amanda, as she noticed the huge mess she'd made. Bowls, spatulas, drips, and splotches of dough were all evidence left behind. She cranked up the music and started to clean. This time Janis Joplin came on the radio, passionate and soulful.

Singing loudly, Amanda wiped down the countertops and organized the bowls in the dishwasher. Belting out the words, even if wildly off-key, felt incredible!

An array of birds perched in Willie's branches.

Is there a convention that I didn't get invited to? she mused. Seriously, where did this flock come from on a gray, rainy day? Wrens, bluebirds and others she didn't recognize.

Shouldn't they be nesting or something? she wondered. A tinge of jealousy, maybe? "Willie has the attentive company of his feathered friends; is he even thinking about me today?" "What tales is he weaving for the gathering of birds?'

Not jealousy, she decided. Probably envy.

Was she that fond of Willie that the birds couldn't be welcomed to share his attention? "Don't be ridiculous, crazy old lady," she scolded herself.

Dragging the wooden easel from behind the couch and clearing out a space near the window, she noticed how decrepit it looked, splattered with paint from someone's artistic endeavors. A few cracks. It had been a yard sale find. Placed in the attic, and never utilized. The fact that it had been used was a plus for Amanda. Recycled wood saved trees. Saving trees didn't make a great artistic idea come to life, though. When purchased, her enthusiasm went astray before it even got started. It'll be different this time, she vowed.

The fresh white canvas, coated with the gesso, stared at her.

She sat and contemplated her options.

The canvas seemed full of hope. Encouragement. Possibility. Potential.

She remembered a six-year old, Sami, from one of her classes during the days of teaching. Sami was tall and lanky, with red-rimmed glasses that always found their way to the end of her nose.

Those glasses were perpetually smudged, no matter how many times we paused to clean them, she remembered fondly.

Sami was undoubtedly an artist. Upon given any project, she dove in with no hesitation. A fearless child with the ability to transform a simple piece of paper and crayons into imaginative pictures, worthy of a blue ribbon.

Amanda smiled as she imagined the little girl's face: innocent, talented. Totally unaware of her own inner resources that could never be duplicated. Amanda expected that child to flourish through her life and vowed to conduct a google search later. Perhaps she was already rich and famous. How exciting, she thought.

Amanda's teaching days were joyful. Her students were such gems, each one with their own personality and hilarious quirks. Little did those children know that the lessons were often her own and unrelated to the curriculum. She recalled embracing those little ones as if they were her own. She lived for those sticky, warm hugs. Empathy was her superpower. Children don't care what you know, she thought. Until they know that you care. There was no doubt that she had cared.

A symphony of birds, heard through the window, brought Amanda back to the corner of the room with the easel. The distraction of days gone by had been welcome and appreciated.

She stared at the blank, untouched canvas, still there.

Her inaction created a strange feeling that she was letting that canvas down.

In that moment, she found it hilarious that she didn't care what people thought of her but letting down this inanimate object was making her feel guilty. How ludicrous.

More time passed and she endured disapproval. The grandfather clock chimed to indicate another hour had slipped by. Zero inspiration.

"Argh," she uttered.

Disappointment crept in, felt in her bones.

The clean, dry brushes and unopened paints remained displayed in the corner by the window where she had cleared out a little nook. Other areas of the room were piled with travel artifacts and magazines. The variety of antique furnishings were filled with belongings. Drawers overflowed with her collections of her lifetime.

Amanda was exhausted. It wasn't from productivity. She was tired from lollygagging. The white canvas remained empty. Her belly filled with scrumptious, spicy rolls, she opted for a long afternoon nap. A serious nap that wouldn't end until the following morning. A kind of rest that happens when procrastinating. Avoidance can lead to long, delicious naps, whether you analyze the reason or not. Maybe it wasn't just her body that was tired, she thought. Maybe her soul, or something deep inside of her, also needed the rest.

A Black Feather

Amanda opened her eyes, confused when she realized she'd slept for twelve hours straight. "I can't remember sleeping this long since I was a teen," she thought as she stretched her stiff body and noticed the bright light of early morning. The sun glowed through the white, cotton curtains that hung from her bedroom window. After days of rain, she was eager to dash out the backdoor to greet the day.

She felt like a child whose summer vacation had just begun. Her heart fluttered with delight, her spirit was rejuvenated. Ignoring the Ayurvedic oils on her dresser, her hairbrush, and other morning rituals, she skipped towards the kitchen. She filled a mug with aromatic coffee and bolted outside, full of vigor and anticipation.

Weeds had sprouted up in the most absurd

places throughout her yard. Several were sticking out of old clay pots she hadn't used in years. The grass needed to be mowed. Her yard was overgrown with ivy and dandelions. Bees swarmed everywhere. The ground was damp beneath her bare feet, a wonderful feeling. Round mushrooms popped up through the weeds. Amanda loved the mystical paradise of emerald green her garden had become.

Savoring the rich, organic Sumatra, she enjoyed her yard-turned-paradise. Wildflowers had popped up in places she hadn't placed seeds. It seemed her yard had transformed into a page from a fairy tale in a few days. She'd always appreciated faeries, sprites, gnomes, and other magical woodland visitors. Amanda now believed they shared her yard. She was pleased at the thought but hoped they didn't become too mischievous! When unsupervised, magical creatures could cause all kinds of chaos.

Long ago, some folks believed faeries played tricks on people, and they were responsible for illnesses. Amanda wasn't sure what she believed, but she was willing to live side by side in harmony with the mystical creatures, just like she did with the bugs and insects.

Maybe I'll leave out some milk and honey in a little bowl, she thought. Just in case they need some nourishment. As a welcoming gesture. I'd love if someone did that for me. Kind gestures often proved more meaningful than grandiose gifts to Amanda.

There was work to be done today. Amanda was convinced digging her fingers into the rich soil, allowing the sun to drench her body: this was the therapy Amanda needed to transform her mood of melancholy and disappointment from the previous day.

She glanced down at her favorite mug with its large sunflower design, a substantial piece of pottery and gift from a cherished friend.

How many times had she found her mug half filled with cold coffee at the end of the day? "Finish your coffee," she reminded herself. Amanda noticed the simple pleasures that filled her life.

Tiny distractions and annoyances were nothing compared to what she had viewed on the news a few nights before. The number of pandemic victims was increasing, and it was highly recommended to continue to shelter in place. Amanda became more fully aware how comfortable she had become in her little corner of the world.

Realizing she was still in her old yellow robe, she enjoyed the final sips of coffee and returned inside to dress for a day of connecting with the earth. Seriously, what could be better? she thought with anticipation. "Dirt-filled nails" always signified a glorious day.

The empathy Amanda had displayed during her years of teaching was not limited to the classroom. In her garden she provided water for the critters that visited her bird bath. She welcomed the ladybugs, who dined enthusiastically on aphids and kept her roses alive and well. The laborious work of the spiders impressed Amanda. She vowed never to disrupt their webs, which she viewed as works of art, wishing she could be so creative. An image of the dusty easel in her living room came to mind, ever so briefly.

Before it was popular public knowledge, Amanda had designed her gardens with bees in mind.

Intentionally drawing them near with irresistible flowers, she knew one of the most important services bees and other insects provide is pollination. She had planted purple and yellow pansies, placed in full sun, along with her fur-like pussy willows in areas of her yard that enjoyed partial sun. There was also milkweed and bee balm that the bees used as a food source. "Insects were here first, by over 300 million years," she liked to remind anyone who would listen. "If it weren't for those little worker bees, we wouldn't have food!'

Maybe I'm a visionary, not just peculiar, she thought. Either way, she was pleased the bees were willing to share the planet with people.

People could be hard to like, after all. They could be selfish. When most viewed insects as pests, people tended to perceive Amanda's care for the little helpers as annoying. Amanda once saw Al spraying chemicals on his peonies.

"What's happening?" Amanda asked.

"These ants are attacking my flowers," Al reported. He was under the impression the ants were an enemy, intentionally harming his precious flowers.

Amanda explained it was their duty to crawl on the emerging buds to encourage the beautiful blossoms to evolve. She hoped her neighbor would understand there was no need to use toxic poison to protect gardens from insects or diseases.

It was an eye opener for the neighbor to admit he had no idea the ants were doing him a favor. "Oh, I thought the ants were uninvited pests," Al admitted sheepishly.

Al was one of the good ones. He was outside in his yard frequently and had a flourishing garden. Amanda wondered why they had not become more friendly over the years.

She noted the nasty chemicals were put aside, at least for that day and she was grateful.

Amanda often thought of the concept of the circle of life, and she wanted to play an intentional part in it all. In her presence, all creatures were safe from harm.

Today, the worms needed her assistance. Through the downpours of the last few days, they had abandoned their underground burrows and crawled everywhere.

Amanda chuckled. "Who knew so many wiggly earthworms lived right beneath where I walk every day?"

Tenderly lifting each worm from the soaked ground, she gingerly placed them in her compost bin. Oliver had questioned this request, but he humored her, building the cedar contraption. It stood through harsh winters and had become one of the most useful items he ever built for her. Bits of lettuce, grass clippings, scraps of carrot peels and coffee grounds became the new environment for the earthworms. Such effortless abundance for these useful creatures, Amanda was aware they would naturally create nutrient rich soil for her gardens.

"Everybody wins today," she announced to Dalilah Belle, smiling.

The day flew by. Dirty hands and bruised knuckles were signs of a fulfilling day. Bits of dried leaves adorned the waves in Amanda's silver hair and the knees of her well-worn jeans were stained green from the grass.

Exhausted, she snuggled next to Willie for a time of well-deserved rest.

She closed her eyes gently as she started the series of deep breaths. Easily she sank into that familiar, tranquil trance: that special place deep within her mind where Willie shared his meaningful stories. Other than the characters in his tales, no one else was invited. It was a sacred place in her mind's eye, in her heart and in her soul where anything was possible.

The scent of burning sage soothed Amanda as she watched a woman use a large black feather to disperse the smoke around a circle of men, women and children. The woman was tall, with long black silky hair. She was confident as her hand directed the smoke. Purifying and cleansing the space was the first step of this fascinating ceremony.

A group of Indigenous people sat in a circle with percussion instruments nearby, and the powers of the Four Directions were then addressed. This ancient shamanic rite honored the powers of creation. The Chieftain first faced the East, then South, then West, then North, inviting each direction to participate and assist in the ceremony. His actions were precise, as if he had performed the rituals hundreds of times. Amanda watched in amazement. Even the children were cooperative and mesmerized.

After the practice of the Four Directions, each participant became silent and set personal intentions for healing and guidance. At that point, the drumming began. Amanda could feel her heart beating to the deep sounds of the drums. The children had small shakers, rattles, and other percussion instruments Amanda could not identify. The drumming was rhythmic and familiar. She was in the middle of a hypnotic regression, experiencing one of the many lives she had lived in a native village. She could see mountains in the distance, a small river just steps away, and copper dust in the air.

The drumming, the chanting, and dancing went on and on. Amanda fell into a deeper trance, completely mesmerized. Her blurred vision became confusing. Groups of people could be seen behind the original circle. Ancestral spirits had arrived. Too many to count. The drumming continued, louder now, with urgency. The ancestors offered unspoken wisdom, protection and love understood by all.

Something was guiding her to participate in the dancing. Her feet pounded on the ground as if she had done this same dance countless times before. Her feet moved to the drumbeat, automatically in a continuous rhythm. She felt connected to the Earth and to her ancestors. The dust arose from the dancing, blending with the residual sage smoke. Energized. Hypnotized. She was absorbing the sounds, as if to memorize them forever, to make them a part of her for eternity. The drumbeats were in her organs, her cells, her bones. She was one with the heart of the Earth.

Others that were nearby looked into her eyes with a knowing: she belonged with them, she was accepted. There was a mutual understanding. Bathed in their protective energy without a single word.

□□□□□□□□□□□□□□□□□□□

A movement on her foot aroused Amanda from a state of deep sleep-dancing. Sensations of the drums lingered. Tired from pulling weeds and doing other yard work, she realized Dalilah Belle was nudging her foot. It was dinner time and Dalilah Belle knew the exact time she was to be fed. Moving towards the back door, Amanda felt the beat of her heart still pounding like a drum. The ancestors remained within her, it was an instinctive understanding that required no explanation, only trust.

By the back door, Amanda found a large black feather. A gift? Coincidence? No, coincidences didn't exist in her reality. Everything had meaning. She held it close to her cheek while Dalilah Belle ate, then placed it on the mantel in the living room where it belonged. Her treasures made their home in the special place. It was her sacred alter, the one place in the cottage that was always dusted, organized and cared for.

Sexy Silvers

The first walk after the Shelter in Place order was lifted brought up unexpected emotions. Amanda and Dalilah Belle strolled through the neighborhood, no destination in mind. It had been months since Amanda had interacted with anyone other than the occasional delivery from Pete or sporadic visits with those who shared their gifts of working the land over at the farmer's market. Amanda appreciated the bountiful harvests. As exchanging money to make her purchases only took minutes, this ritual didn't feel much like socializing, exactly. It was more about having the essentials, and, of course, supporting locals. The Shelter in Place order had only been lifted for a few days, and the community was beginning to go back to what was being called 'the new norm'.

Loads of couples, held hands as they walked,

like they held onto some secret meant for no one else. Neighbors pedaled rusty bikes that, by the looks of them, hadn't been used in years. Children chased one another, yelling unabashedly after being cooped up for so long. Amanda had no idea her community had so many children of all ages. Music streamed from opened windows: a party atmosphere right there in her community. Some adults shyly waved to one another, barely making eye contact. Others were gathered in groups at the corners, animated and laughing, making plans for picnics and dinners. Those at the corners seemed desperate to dive back into their lives.

"The extroverts," she thought timidly.

To be honest, this new norm felt weird. She felt out of place. "Why am I so anxious?" She wondered. She was ready to go back home, even though doing so would cut her walk short.

She had actually enjoyed the time in her own cottage bubble. Gardening, singing, baking. Those special moments with Willie had kept Amanda completely content. She liked her life. It was easy. It was calm. She and Dalilah Belle had an understanding, a rhythm that was working beautifully. It would be okay to keep this kind of living going on longer.

Her new life brought more serenity and acceptance than perhaps she had realized or was willing to openly admit.

"It's strange to think like this. I was the wild one. The extrovert who lived for adventures. Mingling, traveling; those were the good times. I loved all of that. When did I become quietly content all alone?" she thought to herself. It was confusing.

Amanda hurried back home, glad to be back in her cozy and safe cottage.

Checking her phone, which she had forgotten to bring along, she saw six missed calls. All from Catherine.

"Oh, I hope there's nothing wrong," was her first reaction.

Amanda dialed Catherine's number.

"Where have you been?' Catherine said loudly, exasperated.

"Have you filled out the personality profile yet?' Catherine questioned impatiently.

Amanda had no clue what she was talking about, probably because she hadn't been reading her emails lately. Content in her cottage, sealed off from the world, Amanda had dismissed most communication, including the electronic kind. She had been invited to online yoga classes, book clubs, and an array of other opportunities. None seemed interesting enough to pursue. Vaguely, she recalled seeing emails from Catherine, but she assumed her friend was forwarding jokes, recipes, or quizzes. Catherine enjoyed eating up time with such things, which were usually ignored by Amanda.

"I signed us up for a dating site weeks ago. The site uses a scientifically-backed personality profile to match us up to others based on our preferences. Everyone on the site is over sixty. It's dating for the young at heart, like us, Amanda! I already have two potential partners who are interested in me, can you even believe it?"

Catherine was obviously excited. She sounded youthful, with barely a breath between words.

Amanda, on the other hand, was astounded.

"How could you sign us both up for such a personal thing without even asking me?" Amanda implored. "Really, this is so unlike you on so many levels, Catherine. You have obviously not thought this through at all. How can you be so excited about sharing time with complete strangers?"

"I'm not interested in dating anyone. Why would I care about filling out some random personality profile? You want me write about myself online for everybody to see? No way. It's an awful idea. Absolutely not."

Amanda could hear her own voice, whiny and louder than necessary. It felt like someone else's voice was coming out of her lips.

Then silence. Crickets.

Catherine sighed, as if she had something to say, but stopped herself before the words could escape.

More silence, along with a quiet sniffle.

And then, the distinct sound of the phone being disconnected.

Amanda moped into the living room and sat down on the couch with a thump. Dalilah Belle dutifully followed, plopped down by her feet, and yawned. Amanda patted her on the head, enjoying the soft and familiar fur between her fingers. She sat for a long while taking a quiet pause to contemplate.

I suppose I need to take responsibility and get more informed on this situation, she thought. She tried to be reasonably mature, which seemed tricky for some reason.

Amanda opened the multiple emails from Catherine, all sent over the last few weeks. All unopened.

Sexy Silvers to Bring out Your Sparkle was a service that Catherine had been so excited about. She'd sent Amanda pages of testimonials from older folks finding true love. Widows finding companions for trips and dinners. Descriptions of lunch and theater dates.

"Adventure awaits with someone who is the perfect fit for you," she read with more skepticism.

Amanda read the pages filled with testimonials. So many stories; some seemed to have fairy tale endings. She found herself grinning, just a little. She was captivated. Perhaps she would give this Sexy Silvers a little more thought later.

This is the exact type of thing, when much younger, she would have encouraged Catherine to try. Catherine, of course, would have no part in such foolishness back then. She'd have every excuse under the sun why she couldn't possibly participate in anything that could be labeled risky. Amanda recalled the never-ending excuses:

"I just signed up for a new class that will be so hard. My brother is moving and I'm helping him pack. My parents need me to watch after the plants while they're gone."

She would have sent Amanda off with loving wishes and waited patiently for the amazing stories, always living vicariously through her fearless and spunky friend.

Had Amanda been disappointed with the constant refusals from her best friend back then? Perhaps? She couldn't remember. Basically, she had invited Catherine out of respect for their friendship, but expected the answer to be "no", followed by the chain of excuses. It's just the way their relationship was. Catherine was vanilla and Amanda had been the gooey and colorful sundae with a bright red cherry on top.

Catherine and Amanda had both been married for a few decades and lost their spouses within months of one another. They never really talked much about the grief or the loneliness. Their conversations were frequent back then, yet mostly superficial. They exchanged recipes. They talked about taking a painting class together, but it never happened. Amanda told her about the amazing and diverse students in her classes, who were a source of comfort and joy. Catherine had endless tales of her adult children and grandchildren that she was so proud of.

Amanda had loads of friends, but no one close enough to be truly vulnerable with. She dealt with the grief all alone. Or maybe she never really addressed it all. Willie had been her source of comfort, which Catherine wanted to hear nothing about; she had made it crystal clear, again, in their recent phone conversation, "Naming a tree is silly."

Then, along came sweet Dalilah Belle. She had rescued the ball of black fluff shortly after her beloved Oliver's death. A funny pup that gave her a reason to get up each morning. Puppy training and milestones passed quickly. Dalilah Belle had learned to fetch and sit, Amanda thought she was brilliant.

Convinced she was dealing with an exceptional pet, she hung a silver bell on the backdoor and taught the pup to jostle the bell with her paw, indicating when she needed to go out. "Ding-a-ling, Ding-a-ling." It was an advanced skill for a bright pup and the cutest thing ever.

The rambunctious pup that brought joy back into her life was right there at her feet as she thought about those long-forgotten details. Training, snuggling, and being the pup mom had taken up many hours. Hours without Oliver. Days without Oliver. And now, years. It had been a welcome distraction back then. Now, she couldn't imagine life without the adult version of that fluffy ball of fur, who was currently snoring into the rug at her feet.

Amanda glanced over at the forlorn easel, resting in place in the corner.

Unopened paints waited nearby, and the brushes collected dust. She felt as sad as the easel at that moment in time. The easel, however, had no choice to be alone. She was surrounded by large amounts of stuff. "How could I have accumulated so many belongings?" She whispered. Her surroundings made her feel heavy and trapped. Sleep helped her postpone cleaning. Closed eyes made it easy to ignore the unkempt and cluttered mess that surrounded her. It was going to be another early to bed evening.

Rose Gold Glow

Unlike other experiences with Willie, Amanda made the choice to pay a visit early in the morning. Usually, she liked to cozy up to Willie at night. Maybe because of the neighbors. Al, who was a great guy, would probably notify medics if he saw her leaning against her favorite tree, eyes closed and in a trance state. Other neighbors, whom she did not know well had opinions that questioned her sanity. She only knew this because when Casey was little, she once innocently blurted out, "My mom says the neighbors think you're crazy, but I don't care." Amanda had usually chosen to be alone with the friendly tree companion at night when others wouldn't see.

Here it was, broad daylight. She was alert and hoping for reassurance from the steadfast friend about the disturbing discussion concerning online dating. Was she just being old-fashioned and stupid? Was she scared that no one would want to spend time with her?

"Willie, do you have any guidance for me?" She chuckled aloud, recognizing she was seeking romantic advice from an eighty-five foot tree. A tree, she noted, that had not moved from the same location since his tiny seedling was planted in her back yard. Perhaps she was out of touch with reality.

Situating herself on the ground, the bright sun warming her face, she began to relax. Noting a bluebird flying above, she reflected upon the freedom of rootless wildlife, free to roam. Poor Willie, tethered to the soil, never seeing the rest of the world, while the bluebird flew high and observed life from a totally different perspective.

Softening her body as she let his sturdy trunk support her, Amanda resisted the temptation to distract herself with the freedom of the bluebird. She focused back on the solid earth beneath her. Gemini, she thought. Those of us that are air-signs do certainly tend to get distracted easily, don't we? Air, yes: clean, fresh air. Breathing intentionally now.

Deep into her body, she allowed the oxygen to work the magic of the trance. Reaching the depths took her longer today. Breath after breath after breath. Finally, she relaxed into the alpha stage of sleep. Not really sleeping but that stage where the subconscious becomes highly focused, Everything, all noises faded into nothingness. Her eyes remain closed.

There was a green flash of light behind her eyes. It came and went quickly, then turned into a pink haze.

The flash was a mystical, calming shade of rose pink that created a sense of safety.

In that dream-like state rose-colored energy gently surrounded her.

The energy entered her body through her cells. She had no desire to understand it. Emotional for Amanda, she began to shed tears for an unknown reason. Tears seeped through her eyelashes. The sun reflected on the moisture, glowing gold on her cheeks. She was enveloped with love. Love for the creatures in her yard, for the friendships she had, even Catherine who was not currently speaking to her. Most noticeably, she felt an overwhelming love for herself.

She felt a soothing vibration moving through her body. Healing, like a balm of rose-gold silk penetrating through her skin into her body on a cellular level. Calm and peaceful. She was an infant being rocked by a nurturing caregiver, filled with love and safety. Lulled deeper into this sleep-like trance of complete tranquility, healing was taking place whether she agreed to it or not. The process was inevitable and necessary.

She was not able to discern what kind of healing was needed. Her body and mind worked together in perfect harmony. Her heart beat in a slow and rhythmic way, each gentle beat pumping the rose love-energy through her whole system. There was nothing for her to do but to accept it. Resistance didn't occur to her. Why would she resist when she was being offered such a beautiful gift? Amanda felt more love for herself and for the world than she could have ever imagined. The whole time, having been lulled to sleep like a precious and cherished infant, she didn't want it to end. She stayed as long as Willie permitted, and she absorbed the rose-love energy willingly.

□□□□□□□□□□□□□□□□□

She heard the birds chirping. Her stomach told her it was mealtime. Opening her eyes, she continued to feel the love. She thought of the love-based practice she had read about. Ho'opponono originated in Hawaii by indigenous healers and involved reconciliation and forgiveness. She began to send that message to the Universe.

"I love you. I'm sorry," she said. "Please forgive me. Thank you."

With her eyes wide open, she understood each of her mistakes, each transgression, even the ones she had long-forgotten, no longer mattered. She loved herself with full acceptance and now knew she deserved to share that love with others. A partner? A new friend? Deep down, she knew her life was about to unfold exactly as the Universe intended.

When she shifted her body to stand up, she felt something hard and rough beneath her right ankle. Examining and loosening the soil, she found clumps of dried mud. Digging more, she unearthed a handful of mud-caked rocks. She filled her pockets and brought them into the kitchen. She placed them in the sink with a splash of dish detergent and hot water to soak.

She decided upon a creamy warm brie with a juicy cranberry compote and walnuts for lunch. Cranberry juice dripped from her fingers, down onto her arm and splashed onto the table as she prepared her lunch and ate. "Not only is this cottage a mess, but now I'm wearing my lunch." She had found the brie at the farmers market and had been waiting for a special occasion to indulge herself. Was this a way to love herself, through foods she enjoyed? She savored the cheese with crackers and crunchy celery sticks. She had learned from an Ayurvedic class once that a meal should never include both fruit and dairy. This meal obviously broke all the rules, and she left none for leftovers. The meal was just too scrumptious.

Washing the cranberry juice from her hands and arms, she began to rinse off the rocks that had been soaking in the sink. Pink chunks of rose quartz. Raw, rough, and angular. The crystals shone now that they were freshly cleaned. There were about a dozen crystals, in a variety of shapes, and each was about an inch in diameter. Rose quartz was one of the first crystals she had ever collected.

Over the years, she had a large collection that lined her windowsills and dresser. She even kept some under her pillow. She kept smoky quartz crystals in the side pockets of her car, a bright red Mini Cooper, helping to create the grounding and safety her Gemini soul needed to stay focused while driving.

Amanda was delighted with these new treasures. “Rose quartz for self-love,” she thought. “How perfect.”

Willie kept his messages simple enough for her to comprehend. She lined them up on the mantle. Her alter was growing, there was barely enough room to fit anything else. The bright afternoon sun acted as a spotlight for the crystals, like they were on a stage for the world to see yet meant only for Amanda.

Breaking the rules once again, Amanda dug

her spoon into the pint of Ben and Jerry's Cherry Garcia ice-cream. Frozen dairy, adorned with juicy cherries and chunks of chocolate. Whoever made those rules of not eating fruit and dairy together had clearly not indulged in this delectable ice-cream, she thought with a grin. Delish! The creamy goodness was fabulous.

Finally, Amanda sat with her laptop. Reluctantly, she opened to the dreaded Sexy Silvers Personality Profile. Hours passed before she finished. It was like taking a test that you forgot to study for. The pint of Ben & Jerry's was her consolation, providing her with the motivation to click the submit button. She wasn't sure how Catherine would react with the news of Amanda completing and submitting the personality profile. She clicked the submit button and off it went into cyberspace. Or is it called the cloud, she wondered.

With absolutely zero understanding of how the worldwide web worked, she simply trusted it would arrive safely for her own highest good. No need to comprehend the details of the internet, just trust.

As she got ready for bed that night, she noticed the bottles of expensive oils on her dresser. Having sprung for a collection of face and body oils a few months back, she had been excited to be caring for her skin. When the pandemic hit, she certainly had plenty of time to begin the routine of self-care. Anxiety and other excuses had taken over. The initial excitement about having a well-thought out beauty regiment faded into splashing her face with water and occasionally applying sunscreen.

Examining the bottles now, she selected the one designed for nighttime use. It was packaged in a pretty gold and red bottle and was called Manjish Glow Elixir. As she massaged her face with the deeply scented oil, her face became flushed and rosy. She thought of times when she would blush as a teen. The oil felt nourishing on her skin, and she decided she liked it.

"Maybe this will be my personal miracle in a bottle," she thought.

Having dripped a little more than necessary into her palm, she gave her hands and arms the same treatment, because who wants to waste such aromatic goodness on a towel, right? She drifted off to sleep with high hopes of glowing skin and transformation.

Egyptian Lapis

Ting. Ting. Ting.

Amanda's laptop kept making alarming, bell-like noises. She wondered why as she tried turning the volume down, but they kept coming. When she saw the Sexy Silvers notifications her stomach responded by doing what could only be described as spasms of frantic anxiety, along with hot flashes from hell.

Ting. The fact that she'd joined was starting to feel real. Ting. Ting.

"Argh. I'm not ready to face rejection or any other result of this crazy idea." Amanda bolted out of the room. For a mature gal, she impressed herself with how quick her feet moved. "No, I'm definitely not ready."

Leaving the room wasn't far enough. Ting. Ting.

She couldn't escape.

Messages. More messages. Please stop.

"Who are these people sending me messages?" Her curiosity piqued as she cautiously sauntered back into the room. Photos popped up. She couldn't focus. Ting. Ting. "I can't do this now," she groaned. She altered between genuine curiosity and fear. When she noticed her legs were trembling, it was clear the fear was currently winning.

Amanda was desperate. She needed to put an end to this annoyance immediately

Ting. Ting. Ting. "Please, stop", she pleaded with the manufactured piece of metal. "I've made a terrible mistake."

Slamming her laptop closed, she yanked the cord from the wall socket. She stuffed the troublesome thing in her desk drawer. The laptop now sat amid a variety of unidentifiable papers and long forgotten files. At that moment, that piece of metal with its circuit boards and hard drive and other mysterious components was her enemy. It needed to be controlled, or maybe ignored. She felt like she was being attacked, even though she hadn't taken the time to actually read any of the messages. If she had remembered where the old key was stored, she would have locked it in the drawer for her own safety.

"What was I thinking? Stupid personality profile." Amanda mumbled and scolded herself as she walked away from the desk.

Peering over her shoulder at the desk drawer,

she waited to see any signs of her enemy escaping. That thing, as she now referred to her laptop, stayed where she wanted it to stay for days.

The silence gave Amanda satisfaction. A reprieve. Controlled for now.

She busied herself with some shopping. Now that the pandemic had ended, the stores were filled with smiling patrons. The weather was turning slightly cool. Sweater season to this old gal meant a few extra layers and no bra. Technically, she admitted, all seasons meant the same thing during the pandemic, since she was only at home with no judgmental eyes.

Not really a feminist, Amanda was more like an old hippie who preferred the natural feeling of not having wires or scratchy material digging at her skin. Whoever started the trend of such undergarments was probably not a female, she mused.

Still thinking about undergarments, totally unrelated to groceries, Amanda walked through the canned food isle. She thought of her friend Susan-Marie. Not only did Susan-Marie have a bureau filled with fancy undergarments, she didn't seem to mind the discomfort. She loved pink, turquoise, and purple; bonus points if there were sparkles.

Amanda moved disinterestedly down the canned food aisle. She was seeking quick lunch ideas as she drifted back to Susan-Marie, remembering a joke her friend used to tell:

"What has two knees and swims?" she asked. "A two-knee fish!" She always followed the joke with a snort and forced laughter, along with a slap on her black sparkly leggings.

Although it was at least six years ago, it was easy to remember the awkward day her friend revealed her third marriage was about to end. Susan-Marie told jokes, rather than face any kind of conflict. It was her way of deflecting or ignoring situations that made her uncomfortable.

When alone with Amanda, Susan-Marie acted like a different person: friendly, interesting, and even slightly shy. She was the best version of herself when relaxed and in her company, knowing there would be no conflict.

We always enjoyed one another's company, Amanda recalled fondly. "If I were to ever have a sister, I'd want her to be like Susan-Marie."

It was such a relief when Susan-Marie and Elliott met. Finally, a man who deserved the best version of her. He was a kind and generous man. She didn't need to joke when she was with him. He treated Susan-Marie like the precious woman she was.

The moment I met him, I knew her horrible luck with men had come to an end, Amanda remembered. I hear they now have grandkids, which warms my heart. Children always loved Susan-Marie. She was like a magnet to them, and had a lap filled with children at every gathering. They could sense her sincerity. Amanda smiled as she thought about her friend.

Moving around the store, she loaded up on a

variety of delicious teas, including green tea. She had read an article in Prevention magazine claiming that green tea was linked to a lower risk of heart disease. All of those wonderful antioxidants. Plus, the brew warmed her body on chilly evenings - the real reason she'd tossed the box into her cart.

When purchasing her favorite brand, Yogi Tea, she received a few words of wisdom on the tea bag. A special little affirmation awaited with each cup of tea. A simple pleasure. One memorable message: "Empty yourself and let the universe fill you."

She thought about this idea when she sat in silence before bed at night. Meditation was a regular practice for Amanda and the thought of being a part of the universe and being filled with wisdom warmed her heart, exactly as the tea nourished and took the chill from her body.

Local honey was a treat, also. She mixed it with her homemade yogurt for a snack with crunchy nuts. Honey was a favorite, drizzled over warm, savory brie, too. Oh, and with delicious melted butter on her spicy rolls. She could almost smell the nutmeg and cinnamon.

"You can't be my friend if you don't agree that melted butter and honey is heavenly, a natural combination," she had once admitted to Catherine, who happened to agree with her on this topic.

How much butter is too much? For the two friends, it could drip down their arms and still wouldn't be too much. That was the honest to goodness truth, too.

She should know better than to go shopping when hungry. She needed to add butter to her cart, the Irish kind, of course. The French pastry chef, a friend she met in Paris had introduced her to Irish butter. Collette Lynn had said, "If you're going to use butter, and you always should, purchase the best and you'll never regret it."

Moving to the produce aisle as a distraction from butter and honey, Amanda spotted the seasonal vegetables. The root vegetables would become soothing soups for the cooler weather. Once again, Amanda became lost in thoughts as she selected vegetables, making mental notes about potatoes, carrots, scallions and the peppers she froze from her summer garden.

Why not throw in some yams to add sweetness? Thinking about flavors, she remembered that the crockpot was probably buried in the cabinet from last year. It would come in handy soon. She wished she was more organized when storing kitchen contraptions such as her well-used crockpot, waffle iron, and variety of other forgotten blenders.

She was glad she had taken care of her herb garden this year. She had a fleeting thought about asking Dr. Ni if dried cannabis could be added to soups, like she added parsley, sage, and rosemary. Would he laugh? Poke fun at her? Share a family recipe?

She giggled as she thought up a cookbook she could write: *Chill out with Soup*. She cracked herself up as she meandered through the store, chuckling to herself and wondering if Willie Nelson would like some of her special soup.

If the locals could read my mind while I'm shopping, they would probably think I'm crazy, she thought.

She loved that she lived in a small community. She recognized faces of those who had been walking through her neighborhood during the months of the pandemic. Even though she didn't have names to associate with all of the faces, it was a comfort to make eye contact with those that lived close by.

She liked to think that her sweet redhead neighbor, Casey, would be intrigued by her eccentric mind rather than critical or confused. Casey was an old soul and a pleasure to spend time with. Maybe we knew one another in a past life, she thought.

It would explain why they were so comfortable together, despite a half century gap in age.

Amanda moved through the .store in deep thought, her mind jumping around in a familiar manner. When entering the frozen food section, she suddenly became alert. There were her friends: tempting pints of Ben & Jerry's, lined up in neat rows as if to say, "Pick me!" Colorful little pints of joy looked right at her like they had been eagerly anticipating her arrival.

Bourbon Pecan Pie!

(Serious sweetness with a kick, especially when you added your own bourbon!)

Double Almond Chocolate! Chocolate Monkey! Peanut Butter Cup Delight!

(Nuts are protein, correct?) Amanda tossed the frosty treats into her cart with joy.

The pints didn't take up much room.

Triple Toffee Delight! Cherry Garcia! Cannoli! (Sounds delightful!)

Double Mudslide!

(Chocolate is scrumptious)

Sweet Cream Cinnamon!

(So good with oatmeal cookies.)

Ginger Caramel Swirl!

(Could accompany healthy green tea, right?)

Her cart was loaded up in preparation for whatever celebration or emotional roller coaster came her way. Or an ordinary day that turns extraordinary. Thank goodness she had been a girl scout and knew how to be prepared.

After she stashed the groceries in the kitchen where they belonged, Amanda retreated to the living room to rest. She relaxed on the couch with her aching feet propped up on an ottoman and gazed out the front window. The window was opened just enough to feel the change in temperature and enjoy the cool breeze on her skin. A bluebird perched on an outside branch near the shutter she had recently painted blue. She noticed how closely they matched in color.

She had chosen the color for her shutters partly because she loved the interesting name of the paint: Egyptian Lapis. She knew Lapis as a semi-precious gemstone, formally called Lapis Lazuli, and the stone had always intrigued Amanda because it was known to enhance telepathy and other forms of communication.

Geminis loved to communicate. Sometimes they talked too much, which Catherine had pointed out on occasion. Telepathy was something Amanda had planned to study someday. She hadn't been to a gem and mineral show in ages, but finding a good lapis was on her list for the future. The pandemic had slowed all kinds of gatherings down, including the annual gem and mineral show she always attended.

The bird's delicate wings and back reflected the light and could have rivaled any Lapis gem she had ever seen. So pretty, like a blue velvet cape. The belly of the bird was pure white with subtle traces of a deep apricot hue. The bird held a sprig of tiny red berries in her beak. Remaining silent, they communicated. They made eye contact, and Amanda felt her shoulders relax. The two created a connection that can only be described as enchanting.

The bird had been gathering food: juicy red berries. Amanda had just stored her grocery store purchases moments before. Her feathered visitor was now resting, as was Amanda. The two souls, more alike than they were different, sat in a long, comfortable silence. The grandfather clock ticked, but most other sounds melted into the background as she enjoyed the company of the feathered visitor.

She barely noticed the cool air filtering through open window screen and was only vaguely aware of the faint sound of a wind chime from somewhere far off. Maybe it was the copper chime she'd given Casey on her sixteenth birthday. Would her neighbor still have the chime from so long ago, she wondered.

More silence and more peace. This non-verbal, sweet, and uncomplicated communication felt exquisite. The bluebird and Amanda observed one another with curiosity. She was honored to have this unexpected guest. The moments were truly special, and this was probably the most in-depth and valuable social contact she had experienced in weeks, maybe even months.

She recalled a conversation she attempted to have with Catherine long ago. "Animal spirit guides were believed to deliver valuable messages," Amanda explained to her best friend. "Our ancestors and indigenous people relied on animals in all sorts of unique ways. They could provide glimpses of the future. It's so awesome when you're guided to make important decisions. They make an appearance and show up when you need them." The quizzical look on Catherine's face did not indicate any fascination or interest. She made an 'umph' sound, sending a loud and clear message that the conversation was moot, so Amanda gave up on sharing her beliefs.

Now, as she sat in silence, she called upon the bluebird with a simple request, "What do you want to tell me today?"

□□□□□□□□□□□□□□□□□□□

With her eyes closed, leaning her head back on a pillow, she waited. Amanda felt bathed in a calm energy. It was subtle. There was a swirl of golden light. She accepted it. She felt her body melt into the couch. She then saw blue, peaceful light that sent protective warm energy through her body.

"Trust in the divine order," she heard the words. "Everything will flow into perfect alignment."

□□□□□□□□□□□□□□□□□□□

When she opened her eyes, the feathered creature was gone. She sighed with gratitude for the brief experience that helped her to trust that she was exactly where she belonged for now.

"Thank you" she whispered with complete sincerity.

Tie Dye

Every article of clothing Amanda owned was spread out on the bed and draped over the eclectic furniture in her bedroom. Gauzy blouses, yoga pants, overalls, vests with fringe and bohemian style skirts and dresses were scattered on her bed. She also had a ridiculous amount of woven scarves, collected from all over the world. Each held a story or memory. The one she held had come from Greece, made of silk, the color of amethyst. She recalled bartering in a market in Santorini for that gorgeous find. She owned mostly cotton and, as well as other organic, natural fabrics. She surveyed the colorful mess.

"Seriously, where did all of the tie dye even come from?"

She was looking for an appropriate outfit to wear on her first date.

I don't want to look like I tried too hard, she thought. I also don't want to look like a Grateful Dead groupie. Amanda laughed at herself. Am I overanalyzing a simple lunch?

This date was starting to feel more complicated than necessary. Up until this moment, she barely thought about what she wore. She usually dressed for gardening, shopping, and walks. Dalilah Belle had not once questioned her clothing choices, or her practical shoes either.

She pulled into the parking lot of Bryan's Diner in her red Mini Cooper. Bryan's place was one of few restaurants in town that had survived the pandemic.

What do I have to lose? she thought, nervous and excited. It's just lunch. Her fluttering stomach was sending a different message, which she was doing her best to ignore. Smoothing out her dress and adjusting her purse, she was as ready as she'd ever be. Amanda took a deep breath as she stepped out of her car.

A young woman was smoking a cigarette near the back of the parking lot. A flaming redhead with skin of porcelain. Could she be Casey?

What a beautiful coincidence, thought Amanda, as the girl came running over.

"Miss Mandy, is that you?" she asked. No one had called her by that nickname for years.

Embarrassed, Amanda felt obligated to share the fact that she was meeting someone for a date.

"A man named Ronald is taking me to lunch." Saying it aloud felt odd.

"Oh, this is exciting," Miss Mandy. You look so pretty, she gushed as the two friends embraced.

Casey jumped into action. "You need a code word."

"What are you talking about, dear?"

"If you find out he's a jerk or he has bad breath or something gross, let me know with a code word and I'll rescue you," explained Casey.

Amanda laughed and glanced at her watch. "Well, I don't have the time for that, I'm supposed to be in there right now. I'm sure it will be fine. If I'm late he'll think I'm unreliable."

Seated in a comfortable booth with plenty of other lunch-goers, Amanda sipped her water. A few young families were seated nearby. The parents spent a good portion of the time cleaning up spills and reminding the children to sit down. Among several couples, Amanda could easily pick out the pairs that had been married for a long time. Easy conversations with plenty of pauses and silence; no need for constant chatter. She became curious about a couple in the corner as it seemed they were on a date. Stiff bodies, fake smiles, and little breathing between words.

That looks like misery, she thought. I'll be sure to relax and try to enjoy Ronald's company.

What is Ronald going to be like? Casey and her code-word seemed silly, yet it would give her peace of mind in the future. She just might talk to Casey later about the idea.

Ronald was twenty minutes late. What do they call that, she thought. Fashionably late?

Casey was heading toward her table. She breezed by speaking quickly. "He's came from across the street, from Bailey's Bar. His face looks like a beet." she disappeared through the kitchen door.

Ronald was shown to their table by another young employee, not Casey. Her description of Ronald was accurate. Not only was his skin a prominent red, but his pores were huge, and his face glistened with perspiration. Not a glowing, healthy type of glisten, but more like profuse sweat.

Amanda smiled politely as he bent over to say hello, uncomfortably close to her face. She smelled bourbon on his breath. She had a brief thought of the Ben & Jerry's ice-cream in her freezer. What was it called? Bourbon Pecan Pie? She'd rather be home enjoying the ice-cream than smelling the "uor on Ronald's breath.

"Harry", he announced a little louder than necessary, as he thrusted his damp hand into hers. "It's very nice to meet you," Amanda's voice was much softer than his.

I thought his name was Ronald? Amanda was caught off-guard by the introduction.

She couldn't help but notice there was no mention of his tardiness. Amanda amused herself with the unspoken and obvious explanation. "Sorry I was late for this lunch date with you. It's so important to me that I felt the urge to stop across the street to gulp down liquor, and I totally lost track of time. And, by the way, I changed my name since I filled out my online dating profile."

He called himself Harry when he introduced himself. I could be wrong, she thought, but didn't his profile say his name was Ronald? She was perplexed.

"I don't like to use my real name on those online profiles. You never know who might be lurking around and stalking. You can't trust people these days. I like to be smart, really smart, ya' know?"

Leaving no time for Amanda to respond, he launched into a description of his very important government work. She made an effort to listen intently, but the sweat rolling into his huge pores was distracting.

"There's just no such thing as a typical day," he continued. "I work long hours and am busier than almost everyone else at the agency. Over the course of a week, I could be gathering details about illegal activities and undercover work is sometimes necessary. I regularly talk to a variety of intelligence agencies about crucial public affairs. I'm often called to testify for upcoming court cases, ya' know, be an expert witness. No one does the same kind of work I do."

Ronald-Harry took a quick breath to drain his glass of water.

She noticed how short and thick his fingers were. His stunted hands didn't seem to fit the rest of his large body. The sudden quiet startled Amanda for just a second. She glanced at the water dribbling down his chin, mixing with the sweat. Water was a better choice for hydration than bourbon, she thought in passing.

She admired the pretty sweater a lady across the room was wearing. It looked like hand done crochet work, colorful and bohemian with fringe. She'd love to walk over and find out the details but tried instead to focus on Ronald-Harry.

The job description continued. "I'm the only one in the state they call for the type of knowledge I have. I've tried to train others, but they just don't want to put in the work. Too slow. I have a knack of picking up information quickly, so obviously I have no patience for those who ask too many questions, ya' know what I mean?"

This would have been a good time to share a little about her love of teaching, and how people learn when they know the teacher has a genuine interest in them. Nope, he kept talking.

"If I keeled over and died today, there would be total chaos without me there. Let me tell you, those sons of bitches would be clueless. A dead man, kicked the bucket as they say, and a whole office of imbeciles, no idea what they should be doing."

The waitress set a double bourbon in front of him. Apparently, he ordered the drink before he arrived at the table. He lifted the glass with his small, stubby fingers and took a hefty swig, then continued. "In my line of work, there's a twenty-four-seven availability. I got a call at three in the morning the other day to go investigate a possible domestic case related to some illegal stuff I've been looking into, but when I got there I couldn't find any cause to be alarmed. Total waste of my valuable time. They were probably lying to me. They always do, lying to a person of authority is common these days. The paperwork took longer than I expected. Just stayed awake, never went back to sleep. Ya' know, I am fully functional with four hours of sleep. Most people can't survive with such little sleep. I don't know how I do it. People ask me all the time how I can be so alert with hardly any sleep. It's just some sort of superpower I have."

"It's been a long and interesting career, but because I have a top level, I mean the very top kind of clearance, I can't really talk about what I do. I'd love to give you more details. It's fascinating. Really great. I'm top, top level, probably more than anyone you've ever met."

When he picked up the glass, he gave it an impatient shake. He heard the sound of only ice and realized he had emptied it. Ronald signaled to the waitress with a wave of his fat hand for a refill. She noticed he was sweating more now.

It wasn't that Amanda wanted a beverage, but it would have been cordial for him to offer her one. Plus, the woman with the beautiful crocheted top was on her way out the door. If she could've gotten the information about that top, the time here with Ronald-Harry wouldn't feel wasted.

With his second drink almost gone, the waitress dropped off a couple of menus. This date had already felt like an eternity. Amanda began mentally listing tasks she could be using this time for instead of sitting at this table with Ronald-Harry. She could be cleaning out the refrigerator. Maybe folding the load of laundry that was still in the dryer. Even organizing her spice cabinet seemed like a chore that would be more enjoyable than listening to Ronald-Harry talk. The best choice was sitting quietly in her own peaceful home eating some Ben & Jerry's ice-cream, just not the one with bourbon in the name.

The menu at this quaint community restaurant had not changed in all the years she lived in town. She'd already decided to order the shrimp salad. A bit spicy, not too much mayo, and always delicious. Bryan's Cafe was known for their shrimp, it was the best around. She had tried to duplicate the recipe, but to no avail. At one point she was convinced it had a sprinkle of rosemary, but that hadn't tasted quite right. Ronald-Harry selected ribs, garlic mashed potatoes, and said no to the salad or more water.

Amanda struggled to smile, the combination of bourbon and garlic an unpleasant thought. She sipped her water, wondering if he wanted to hear about her teaching career. Or maybe her garden. Or funny stories about her smart and obedient Dalilah Belle. No way would she share sweet details about Willie, of course. That was her special secret.

He didn't seem interested in even inquiring about her. He became belligerent when the food arrived a minute later. Amanda noted the lightning-fast service and was about to compliment the young waitress when Ronald-Harry blurted, "This doesn't look like a full rack to me. Are you feeding a child or a *man*?"

As he raised his voice, sweat and saliva dribbled down onto his plate. "What's this? An appetizer portion or something?"

The waitress did not reply but looked at Amanda. Amanda was sure she'd noticed the shocked and disapproving look on her face. They shared a brief moment of nonverbal connection and compassion for one another.

"For these prices, I should be getting the whole damn pig."

Casey appeared out of nowhere. "Miss Mandy, your neighbor just called, and Dalilah Belle got loose somehow, running out on the street. She knew you'd want to know!"

Partially startled by the authentic sounding story, Amanda paused for a nano-second. Then she realized, bless her heart, Casey's rescuing me! She stifled a giggle.

"Oh, thanks, I better go get her," said Amanda. "I can't thank you enough. I'd be heartbroken if anything happened to her." Grabbing her purse, Amanda avoided eye contact with Ronald-Harry and bolted for the door. It was tempting to look back to see what he was doing, but the thought of him with BBQ sauce on his red, sweaty face made her stomach turn.

Amanda rushed out to the parking lot. Casey stood by her car holding a brown paper sack. "Here's your shrimp salad, Miss Mandy. I added some curly fries and a side salad. I think you'll love our amazing strawberry cheesecake, too," she said with a grin. "Might as well have him pay for a full lunch, right?"

"Oh, Casey thanks, for the food, but more importantly thanks for your help. I don't know how I would have managed to stay at that booth any longer. What an experience!".

"He's an asshole" Casey summed it up succinctly with shake of her red curls. They both nodded in agreement with a chuckle.

The long, sweet and restorative embrace came next, two kindred spirits. Decades apart in age, but the number of trips around the sun had no relevance. They were two fiercely compassionate women spanning several generations, and they loved one another in a way that required no explanation.

Her Mini Cooper transported her home safely as she accepted the obvious fact that Ronald-Harry-Bourbon-Garlic man was not meant to be in her life.

Placing the freshly ironed linen dress back in her closet, Amanda noted the vibrant, tie dye frenzy of clothes strewn around. Ronald-Harry took no notice of what I was wearing, but it did feel good to dress up a little. I must say, though, I looked okay for an old gal. I still wish I had more information about the pretty crochet top the woman at the cafe was wearing.

Amanda was glad to be home. She ate her meal by the fireplace. The shrimp salad did not disappoint. Still not able to put her finger on the exact ingredients, she vowed to figure it out someday. Not today, though. She saved the side salad for tomorrow and crunched on the curly fries. The first Sexy Silvers date was certainly not a success. It was an experience Amanda did not wish to repeat. She had hoped for some companionship, but instead was bathed in bad breath and perspiration. She considered Casey's description and laughed out loud. "Goodbye, Ronald-Harry-Bourbon-Garlic man", then added "asshole" at the end for her long friend.

As the day ended, she included a scoop of Red Velvet Cake ice cream to enjoy with the cheesecake. She ate slowly and with deliberation.

I'm just glad it's over and Casey came to my rescue, she thought. What a darling girl.

Dalilah Belle watched her eat, with no recollection of being loose in the street or being used as an excuse to escape from Ronald-Harry-Bourbon-Garlic man.

Catherine's going to get a kick out of this, she thought. But it'll have to wait until tomorrow. She planned an early evening filled with self-care and calm.

The day had been long with the anticipation of the date, along with the unexpected ending. Amanda was enormously grateful for Casey. She found the asshole statement hilarious, considering in some ways, she still thought of Casey as a child.

Feeling emotionally drained, she opted for a long, hot bath with lavender essential oil, Epsom salts, and candles. She turned on some of her favorite music.

Elvis sang "Can't Help Falling in Love" to her in a deep masculine voice.

Her beloved Oliver had indulged her with the claw foot bathtub, and she enjoyed it now just as much as when it was first installed. The warmth seeped into her as she relaxed, finally able to laugh off the Ronald-Harry incident, and to be grateful for her cozy home. She appreciated the solitude that came with living there with Dalilah Belle. She didn't mind the variety of critters that frequently visited her magical yard. Did she really need anything else? No, she did not. Not right now.

A- Award

The next morning, the light was perfect in the living room, and Amanda's bluebird painting was coming along nicely. She was working on the red berries in the little beak. She added lighter shading, attempting to make the berries appear shiny and juicy like she remembered the real ones looked.

Amanda focused intently on this little masterpiece because it gave her a sense of accomplishment. It was the kind of focus that allowed outside thoughts to fade away. Only her paints and brushes mattered. She also attributed her mental clarity to the fluorite crystal nearby. Knowing crystals possessed metaphysical properties renowned for enhancing quality of life, she had purchased the beautiful fluorite point a few years prior. The crystal was a gorgeous find with purple and light green swirls. She kept it on the windowsill nearby where it shimmered in the sunlight like a supportive cheerleader.

She recalled the Egyptian Lapis paint that adorned her shutters and wondered if any local gem and minerals shows were planned.

Lapis Lazuli would be nice to add to my collection, she thought. Its color was close to that of her bluebird friend, and the crystal was known to be great for communication. Who knows, she pondered. Maybe I'll go on a date with someone who I can actually talk to and practice those communication skills.

Crystals were one of her passions. Some considered collecting the metaphysical rocks more suitable for liberal-minded hippie-types. Amanda's close friend, a mathematician who worked as a consultant on projects, who was right-brained as they come was her crystal buddy. She sent a quick message to her friend, Marcia, about Lapis Lazuli. Marcia was Amanda's friend who regularly accompanied her to gem and mineral shows. She had a good eye for bargains, as well as for unique crystals.

While attending these shows, Amanda often ran into plenty of other people she knew. Crystal collectors were a special breed of folks; some would say unconventional. Amanda believed her friends had good energy and that they too believed the best gifts came from the earth. Plus, crystal shows are my favorite place to show off my tie dye collection, she mused.

Amanda was at peace in that corner of her

living room. Whether it was because of the special message from the sweet feathered visitor, or the actual painting, she had no idea. Painting provided a certain contentment for her. Standing in front of the old easel with paint on her hands and the velvety bluebird looking at her with approval was therapeutic. Typically, Amanda could care less about what people thought of her. She lived by a quote attributed to Eleanor Roosevelt: "Do what you feel in your heart to be right, for you'll be criticized anyway. You'll be damned if you do, and damned if you don't."

Today, however, the sense of approval from the bluebird gave her a glimmer of hope for her future.

Lost in her bubble of creativity, Amanda tried to ignore the phone when it rang. She loved working on the painting and didn't want to be interrupted. She yearned to continue concentrating on the little bluebird. The phone rang for a third time and became harder to ignore, despite her best efforts.

She knew it would be Catherine on the phone, waiting to hear details about her date. Amanda was certain Catherine wouldn't stop calling until she gave in and picked up the phone. Friends for decades, Amanda knew Catherine was predictable, and persistent. There was no point in delaying the inevitable.

"I suppose being smart and cautious by using a different name isn't such a bad idea," Catherine lamely defended Ronald-Harry-Garlic Breath-Asshole.

She was making an obvious effort to be positive, and Amanda knew how much Catherine wanted this whole endeavor to work out. That initial conversation about Silver Singles had been awkward and frustrating, but they got over the conflict and remained best friends. They even referred to the incident as the, "Bring out your Sparkles" argument.

"Well, I commend you for showing up and enduring the torture, Amanda. I wish it had been a better experience. I'm so glad Casey was there to rescue you." Catherine was pleased that Amanda had taken some risks regarding the online dating idea. She was proud that she had surprised Amanda. Catherine was feeling quite bold and desperately wanted the dating to end as an epic experience for them both. "The next date has to be better, right?" said Catherine with an effort to encourage Amanda not to give up.

They talked about how the roles had reversed and Catherine was secretly thrilled Amanda noticed her courage. "I'm moving into my later years with some gusto" Catherine declared. It's good you're over the initial shock that I've transitioned into a woman who no longer lives in fear." She didn't want to admit she had been heart-broken and crushed the day Amanda told her Silver Singles was an awful idea.

Amanda knew her best friend well enough to know that Catherine had taken long, painful days to fill out her personality test, analyzing each question, even dreaming about her responses at night. Amanda admired her friend for this obvious challenge. She was aware that her own care-free attitude from her younger years was changing now. Amanda loved the idea of them both finding a companion. She observed with great interest as her best friend began to crawl out of the hiding space she'd created for herself. It was fascinating and beautiful. Amanda was proud of Catherine.

The Ronald-Harry-Garlic Breath-Asshole conversation continued. "Oh, not pungent garlic," said Catherine. "Eww. And messy ribs?"

"Seriously, could he have possibly chosen a more obnoxious lunch, even if he tried?" Catherine said emphatically.

They were hysterical to the point of snorting!

"He was vile. Yuck. Short stubby fingers and a red, sweaty face. Really gross." Amanda explained with a look of disgust on her face.

They laughed even harder, sharing facial expressions that could rival an actor auditioning for a horror movie.

"Maybe he should write a book about his very, very, important job at three in the morning, since he doesn't need any sleep. He'd have loads of time to devote to the endeavor. What a fascinating book it would be. The title could be, *I'm Very, Very, Very Important,* and there could be a photo of a whole damn pig on the cover." Catherine exclaimed with a snort.

"Honestly, he talked about keeling over and

dying?" asked Catherine. "Just plopping onto the floor at work or what? What a great conversation starter. Was the second date going to involve planning a funeral?"

Ronald-Harry-Bad-Breathe-Man kept them joking on the phone like teenagers.

They agreed that if there were ever a Silver Sparkle Asshole Award, Ronald-Harry would be the honored recipient. They only hoped they wouldn't have to award a second place anytime soon, or ever.

"Do you think it's possible to meet a partner online?" questioned Catherine.

The phone conversation steered away from Ronald-Harry now. Amanda reminded Catherine of Susan-Marie and Elliott. Elliott was a musician, the kindhearted soul that would love Susan-Marie forever. It wasn't just flowers and generosity. It wasn't that he was handsome. He had transformed their friend into who she was meant to be all along. He was accepting and loved her exactly as she was. The version that only her closest friends had been introduced to in private. It was a beautiful thing. Now, thanks to Elliott, Susan-Marie was truly and genuinely happy.

Yes, anything is possible. The two friends agreed that it is conceivable online dating would end well for them too.

Literature

Amanda carried kitchen scraps out to the compost bin early Sunday morning. It was frosty outside, but the compost pile was visibly warm. Waves of heat wafted up from the dark humus. This was another reason to visit the local market and buy loads of fruits and vegetables. All the scraps created what she referred to as *black gold*, The nutrient-rich end result of her diligence helped the earth and provided the organic soil to be used in her flower beds, pots and vegetable gardens next spring. "My gardens are going to love this soil." She'd harvest luscious fruits, healthy vegetables, and even aromatic herbs.

She also introduced some worms that year. It turned out that adding worms to compost was beneficial. An owner at Steven's Garden Shoppe had shared his secret with her. He even donated a few of his worms to her endeavor. "The red wigglers will definitely speed up the process of decomposition. You're going to see a big difference when you introduce them into your compost bin." Steven claimed with authority.

This sounded like a marvelous idea to Amanda. Her red wigglers now lived in luxury, chewing down the bountiful kitchen scraps and living the good life.

She thought of the cannabis seedlings Dr. Ni promised her for spring planting. She'd have to do some research to find out if they preferred sun or shade. Amanda had dried sage for years. The tightly woven bundles were tied with basic string and used for smudging her home and precious property. She'd learn how to dry her new plants too, promising Dr. Ni to be careful and cautious. She was looking forward to the medicinal properties the seedlings would provide. Amanda had been honored that Dr. Ni trusted her and was willing to share so generously. Feeling content, she prepared for her time with Willie.

Amanda placed the wool blanket down by Willie. It was too cold to sit on the ground that day, but Amanda didn't want to miss out on the chance to spend time with her ancient friend. The blanket kept her body warm as she scooted closer to his sturdy trunk that she found so welcoming. What sort of interesting message would he share today?

Amanda relaxed her body and began to breathe cool, fresh air into her lungs, her body, and soul. Releasing the air, long and slow, she fell into a beautiful state of rest. Further and further down she fell. So calm, like sleep, only better.

□□□□□□□□□□□□□□□□□□□

In front of her she saw a stairway with beautifully carved handrails and wide steps. Taking her time, she stepped down, noticing the beauty that surrounded her. She was in a garden with tall flowers of orange and yellow. Day Lilies swayed in the breeze. The yellow goblet-shaped flowers, primroses danced with the day lilies as if they were little children playing, oblivious and innocent. Delicate white peonies in full bloom graced the side of the stairs, close enough for Amanda to take in the intoxicating fragrance.

Amanda felt her body soften more now; she relinquished control, allowing Willie's trance to guide her. She trusted him completely. Feeling deeply calm and relaxed, she stopped to rest on the final step, using the ornately carved railing to steady herself. Looking around, she saw that her surroundings had transformed into a beautiful pastoral setting. Rolling green hills and wide-open space: it was breathtaking.

Two large trees supported a white, velvety hammock. She lied down gracefully, with her head on a soft pillow, and drifted deeper into the state of tranquility. The breezes created a soft rocking motion. Lulled into what felt like sleep, she dreamed of a meadow with wildflowers all around her. There was no beginning and there was no end.

This idyllic place was for angels, it seemed. She watched as the beings of light moved in quiet harmony to unheard music. Dressed in filmy white gowns, the energy was like she had never known. Was this Heaven?

The volume of the outside world was silenced. She could hear only the heartbeat of this place, soft and gentle. The angels glided and soared through the meadows. Amanda was not one of them. She felt as if she was observing through the window of a poem, fortunate to see with her heart, rather than her eyes. A piece of literature that existed for centuries but was written for her alone.

What was this poem? Who was the poet? She rested in the meadow, aware of the angels, and still hearing the earth pumping the graceful energy into the universe. The heartbeat was steady and loving.

She couldn't separate it from her

own rhythmic heart. She didn't want to. Her human heart synchronized with the planet in a duet, accompanied by the music of her soul.

Upon awakening, she longed for the open spaces. There was freedom in the wide spaces. She looked for the beings of light, whom she had called angels, but there was only Willie and herself. Dalilah Belle sniffed around the fallen autumn leaves, but there was no one else to be seen. She sat under her old friend, the oak, and noticed how the sun bounced off his scarlet and golden leaves. The light was soft and peaceful, like those primroses in her dream. She noticed the distinct fragrances of the flowers, not knowing whether the sweet scent was in her imagination or not.

Gathering up the woolen blanket and moving towards her cottage, she saw a white blossom on the ground. A single cut flower, laying on top of a small book. A peony! She took in the delicate fragrance with deep appreciation.

A gift, she thought.

Amanda placed the cut flower in a vase and

found just the right spot on the mantel. Sitting down by the fireplace, warmed by the golden embers, she looked at the book: The Odyssey by Homer.

Amanda read the poem, believed to be written sometime in the eighth century. It was a timeless work of literature: a story of compassion, and loyalty. She read descriptions with details that mimicked the field in her dream with Willie.

The angels she read of existed in a place thought to be the afterlife, where souls danced. When she closed her eyes, she could still see them: the light-filled white gowns, the graceful, childlike movements. Utopia. Human emotions like regret, fear, and sadness did not exist there. Only love. Powerful and pure love that Amanda had not known existed. She longed to be back there, among the angels and bathe in that pure, loving energy.

This is my life, Amanda reminded herself. It's right here, in my home. In this community. She struggled to bring herself back to the reality of the present moment. It was in this cottage my beloved Oliver took his final breath, she remembered.

That last day with Oliver seemed like a bad dream. Over time she accepted that he was gone from this earth. Yet she felt his presence, always near, and trusted he was looking after her. He would be proud of her independence. He'd praise her painting. He would disapprove of Ronald-Harry and be tickled with Casey for coming to her rescue.

Amanda was grateful for the precious time they had together.

Dalilah Belle moved closer to Amanda's feet, enjoying the glow of the fire.

The movement brought her back to the present moment even more now. It's no Utopia, she thought. But it's a decent life.

The embers were warm and the exact temperature she liked. Her eyes wandered to the little bluebird painting. It wasn't complete, but she was getting close. She wasn't ready for her afterlife. Not just yet.

She had ice cream to enjoy. She had a painting to finish. And, the following day, she had another date!

Carrot Cake

Bryan's Diner had become a regular hangout lately. The week before, Amanda had met Catherine for an early dinner.

"At some point I vow to figure out the recipe for this fabulous shrimp salad," Amanda said as they ate. There was no mention of Ronald-Harry-Garlic-Man, although when they glanced at the menu, both women paused briefly at the ribs with garlic mashed potatoes. He wasn't worth their time.

Catherine told her about her three-year old twin granddaughters and all of their adorable antics. "Little cherubs with a bit of an attitude," she'd described them. "The way they put those chubby hands on their hips when they're mad is hilarious. The girls can sing 'I'm a Little Teapot' now, too. It won't be long before they're old enough for ballet classes. I can't wait to purchase their first tutus."

Catherine glowed when she spoke about her grandchildren. She was meant to be a Nana more than anyone. She was patient and reliable. No matter how many times the girls wanted to sleep at Nana's, she never refused. She fed them gourmet breakfasts including green eggs and ham and pancakes in every shape imaginable. Amanda was delighted to see Catherine so animated and passionate about those little ones.

Amanda told Catherine about James - a new Sexy Silvers guy she's been chatting with. "I'm giddy, like a teen. He sounds like the opposite of Ronald-Harry- Garlic Breath-Asshole! We planned our get-together weeks ago. I can't believe it's in three days. It snuck up on me. From what I can tell from our phone conversations, he seems polite and organized. Even punctual. He might be slightly introverted, but that's not a problem, really. Much better than loud and pushy, as far as I'm concerned."

"Our phone conversations have been pleasant. No signs of any disgusting characteristics like Ronald, the asshole. I'm feeling optimistic about this one," Amanda admitted.

"Are you much of a drinker?" She had asked casually during a phone call.

"I don't keep alcohol in my house. I sipped on a glass of champagne on New Year's Eve," he had explained. "It was mostly out of obligation to the host of the party. We all watched the ball drop on television and talked about New Year's resolutions."

Amanda was inquisitive, yet cautious. So far,

she trusted this man, James, to be giving honest responses. “Well, what was your resolution for this year?” Amanda had been curious.

“I decided to meet someone to spend time with,” he had responded.

Amanda was intrigued with this resolution and wondered if she would be that someone for James.

Pulling out the same pale gray linen dress, she chose not to over-analyze her clothing choice. It was soft and comfortable. She selected a pretty silk scarf she purchased in Paris. She wore silver dangling earrings. Considering the cooler weather, she found a cashmere cardigan in her bureau that matched the silk scarf. Shades of dark teal and violet against the pearl gray dress felt suitable. She was ready. No fussing, she had promised herself.

When she arrived at Bryan’s Diner, Casey was waiting at the entry.

“Okay, Miss Mandy, I’m going to keep an eye on your table. You’re right about the codes, though. We don’t need a secret word. I’ll know if anything looks weird," she explained.

Casey was an intuitive young woman. Amanda trusted she would sense any vibes that indicated she might need Casey’s help. Telepathic communication, why not?

They selected a table in the corner. Amanda faced the doorway, so she’d be able to see James arrive.

She felt at ease and more confident than she had in a long time. Knowing Casey was watching out for her helped her look forward to spending the evening with James. Amanda hoped there was real potential for a lasting friendship, or maybe more.

James arrived moments after Amanda had been seated. She smiled at his punctuality.

"Good evening, I'm James," was all he said before taking his seat.

"Great to meet you, James. I'm Amanda, as you already know." Amanda chuckled aloud, slightly embarrassed. She'd bungled the introduction by stating the obvious, perhaps even sounding stupid. He didn't seem to notice.

James was dressed in a plain white shirt and black polyester pants. No particular style. He appeared to be younger than Amanda expected, almost youthful. With a quick glance at his hair, she detected little to no gray. He sat rigid, looking like the top collar of his shirt needed to be loosened so he could breathe more easily. They both had water with lemon. He placed his napkin dutifully on his lap, as if he had been schooled at a young age on the proper etiquette of dining.

When he began to talk, Amanda could see the fine lines around his face. She was glad. It appeared he had been honest in his profile information concerning his age.

"This is a good place to meet because the parking lot is convenient, don't you agree?" he asked.

"Yes, it's easy. Plus, the food is excellent, "she added.

"I hope they don't use too much salt. I've noticed that at restaurants lately," he stated while he scrunched his face like a child who doesn't like his dinner. Amanda responded with a vague nod.

"I'm glad the weather is finally cooling off. The heat this summer was unbearable," he said with a high-pitched voice.

Amanda, who happened to adore warm weather, smiled politely, and added, "Well, there's a good reason why Vitamin D is called the sunshine vitamin. It's helpful to be exposed to the sun." James didn't respond verbally or with any facial expression.

She struggled to see any noticeable personality traits in James. There was nothing to like or dislike. Neutral, so far, she thought. She felt safe, which was a plus. Amanda was hopeful, as the evening continued, that James would begin to relax and open up more.

"I'm glad they don't have meters in the parking lot," he announced randomly. "The library has those and it's annoying to have to bring quarters."

Amanda couldn't think of a response, so she remained quiet and nodded.

"Do you have a pet?" Amanda asked eagerly, ready to share some Dalilah Belle stories.

"No, I have allergies," he said grimly. "Especially to dogs."

Being with James made her feel sleepy. His

voice was monotone and whiny, sounding like a teen girl asked to read aloud in a classroom: reading the words, embarrassed, doing as she was told just get it over with. Although it was not late, Amanda was struggling to keep her eyes open. She planned some coffee with dessert to give her a boost. Her mind drifted, curious to see the dessert menu, which unlike the entrees, tended to change often. Dessert always made Amanda happy.

Amanda and James ate their meals in a comfortable silence. He had grilled chicken.

"Sauce and salad dressing on the side, please. And no ice in my water."

Amanda ordered a dish with swordfish meatballs, and charred leek salsa verde.

"This is delicious," she told James. James didn't remark on whether he enjoyed his meal or not.

The food had perked Amanda up a little. Casey passed by several times, stopping to refill their water glasses, an incognito observer. The sun had set and candles were lit on the table. Amanda was hoping he'd say yes to the dessert menu so she could order coffee, and maybe they would have some interesting new choices of pie or some other tempting treat.

It wasn't until James referenced The Odyssey that he finally gained her full attention. Amanda had lost her train of thought, still thinking about that much needed coffee, when James recited, "There is a time for many words, and there is also a time for sleep."

Amanda recognized the words from the epic poem and grinned widely. "You're quoting the Greek poet, Homer!"

Suddenly there was a new level of interest in James. This conversation could easily go from shallow to enlightening, she mused with a glimmer of new hope.

Their waitress appeared and offered dessert.

"No, thank you," he told the waitress firmly, refusing before Amanda had even had a chance to suggest coffee. She was disappointed when he didn't look her way to inquire if she wanted anything.

James had sparked an ever-so-small interest with his reference to Homer. But within minutes she realized the date was coming to an end. He ended their time together abruptly, speaking in the same familiar, polite manner as he had during their introductions. He gave her no chance to discuss Homer or anything else at all.

"It's getting late and I believe we can say our goodbyes now, Amanda."

James stood, nodded, and headed for the door. He had signed the check and walked away, leaving her at the corner table, candles flickering.

What the hell just happened? Amanda thought, astounded. It was far from an enlightened conversation, as she had briefly hoped for, and he was almost to the exit door now.

Amanda expected him to turn and wave. To acknowledge her existence in some tiny way. But he did not. He took his plain white shirt, black polyester pants, and walked stiffly out the door, eyes forward.

She thought of the time when she walked out of the same door, leaving Ronald-Harry alone. Did he expect a gesture of some kind? No. He was occupied by ripping BBQ'd animal flesh with his teeth, some of it smeared on his sweaty face, she concluded. Amanda shuddered at the gross image in her mind: his small, pudgy, hands covered in red sauce.

She began to question if James was disappointed. Maybe he had been tired or something else she had not detected in his monotone voice. She wasn't certain if this was a rejection, or if she was relieved that he was gone. It was a tough call. She didn't remember dating being so confusing when she was younger.

Moments later, Casey arrived with a tray of two cups of coffee and two generous slices of carrot cake adorned with mounds of cream cheese frosting and sprinkled with nutmeg. Amanda's mood instantly elevated, and they ate in a comfortable silence. The cake was delicious. Amanda realized the food she had ordered for dinner was the highlight of the date, rather than the time she'd spent with James.

The dessert disappeared quickly, with looks of unspoken appreciation between the two.

"Were you bored out of your skull? He had

that annoying robot voice." Casey burst into laughter. "Oh, Miss Mandy, I thought you were going to fall asleep right here at the table! He even left without asking if you wanted dessert or leaving a tip. What a dweeb," she added with cake crumb on her chin.

Amanda chuckled. "I couldn't have said it better myself, dear."

"We seriously need to find you a new dating site, Miss Mandy."

Cowboy Hat

Amanda awoke from a restorative sleep with her favorite blanket wrapped around her body, keeping her cozy and safe. The sparkling sunlight from the window was enchanting. She could have stayed in bed all day. The use of the purple weighted blanket was her favorite nighttime ritual during the cooler season. Soft and comfortable, the blanket felt like a hug. She always slept better with that blanket. One of the first purchases she had made after Oliver had gone, somehow, it helped make the cold and lonely nights bearable. After years of use, Amanda associated the best nights of sleep with that plum weighted blanket and regarded it as her best purchase ever.

Lingering in her comfortable bed on a cold morning seemed like an indulgence she deserved. She thought about the plans for the day, going over a short mental list. Grocery shopping was top of mind, but nothing much else besides perhaps reading. The cottage certainly could use some organizing and de-cluttering, but she would continue to procrastinate and ignore the mess.

She thought about returning Catherine's call. Amanda was sure dear Catherine was anxious to talk about the Silver Singles progress, but she had nothing interesting to report. She hadn't even opened her laptop in weeks.

She couldn't really think of a way to describe the date with James. Over the rejection now, she'd come to think of it as a blessing in disguise. He hadn't seemed like a good fit at all. The brief quoting of Homer had been the only hopeful point of the entire night, and even that had led to disappointment. Admittedly, the carrot cake with Casey had been awesome, but that had nothing to do with James. Dessert with him would have been just as boring as dinner.

Who wants to waste scrumptious carrot cake with a boring man anyway? she mused.

As she began to stir in her cozy bed, she noticed the exquisite silence. The quiet was comforting and peaceful. Peeking out the window, a blanket of sparkling snow covered the ground. Several inches had fallen while she slept, transforming her yard and quaint community into a scene of pure serenity.

Amanda recalled teaching her students about snow and how it absorbs sound waves, quieting the outside world. She had been a creative, spontaneous teacher, so when the weatherman had predicted snow, she taught the impromptu lesson. The children had been excited about the chance of a snow day and, to be honest, so had she. After the lesson, they had created large snowflakes using white paper and silver glitter. They had transformed the classroom windows into a sparkling blizzard.

As she waited for Catherine to answer her call, Amanda relaxed with a cup of coffee. As a celebration of the snow, she liked to add ice cream to her coffee. This had been a ritual for many years. That morning she chose a dollop of Ben & Jerry's Mudslide and plopped it into her favorite mug of aromatic Sumatra. Spoiled with the awesome choices, Ben & Jerry's was the only brand she would consider. At any chance to celebrate, she always included Ben & Jerry's ice cream, even when it was freezing cold outside.

Catherine's voice came through the receiver. "Well, you're not really telling me much about the date. A white shirt and black pants don't seem like enough reason to be so negative. Can you describe James by more than just what he was wearing?" Catherine was trying to make this whole Silver Singles thing work for Amanda.

Amanda thought long and hard.

"Are you there?" Catherine inquired.

"Yes, I'm trying to think of a good way to describe James, so you understand. Imagine you leave a can of generic lemon-lime soda on the kitchen counter overnight."

"Well, okay," Catherine played along.

"Now, the next morning, you pour it into a clear, plastic cup."

"I would never drink that," Catherine replied. "It'll be warm and flat."

"Exactly." Amanda nodded emphatically even though Catherine couldn't see her.

Catherine sighed. "Wow, was he really that dull?"

The conversation continued, but not about James. "Did you see how perfectly pristine the snow was early this morning?" Amanda inquired.

"Yes, so beautiful. The twins have a new sled. It's one of those saucer ones. They'll have a blast today, I'm sure. I hope that sled is safe for them. I'm sure they'll be fine. I wish it wasn't so cold, though. They'll need mittens outside for sure. Their little hands could get frostbite, after all. I'm so glad I bought those snowsuits on sale last year. I got the bigger size and it was a good choice. Do you remember those suit snowsuits I showed you? The ones with polka dots? They've really grown, and the snow pants are the exact length for them now." Catherine explained with enthusiasm.

Amanda sipped her delicious coffee, half-heartedly listening to Catherine's lengthy story. Catherine tended to repeat herself, and Amanda could recite many of the stories herself, but she remained polite. Those stories meant the world to Catherine and Amanda obliged her by being the recipient once again, as good friends do.

"Well, I've got to head to the grocery store," said Amanda, finally concluding the chat after heroic patience.

"Do you think your tiny car will be safe to drive in the snow?" Catherine warned.

"Oh sure," said Amanda. "German engineering. I'll be perfectly fine."

On days like this one Amanda wished she had a garage. Scraping the ice and snow off her car seemed to take forever. The hat and gloves she wore were toasty, so it wasn't uncomfortable, just time consuming. One of the joys of being a senior citizen was that everything seemed to take a little longer.

Her hat, a Peruvian Chullo, and matching gloves, were adorned with every color of the rainbow. The warm hat's earflaps were funky, one was slightly longer than the other. She referred to it as her cattywampus fashion. Amanda loved the handcrafted set made from vicuña, also known as alpaca wool; it made her smile. She had purchased the combo on a trip long ago and still wore them, even though the winters in her community were certainly no comparison to the freezing mountains of Peru. The set she purchased was so colorful, you could see her a mile away, which had appealed to her during her youthful adventure. The funny looking earflaps were the brunt of many jokes over the years, yet that never stopped her from wearing it.

Amanda's Mini Cooper hugged the roads easily as she praised the German engineering and sung to Bob Marley on the way. The parking lot was virtually empty, and she snagged a space right next to the front door. She had a feeling this was going to be an awesome day.

She entered the grocery store in her unconventional hat carrying her reusable bags. She was on a mission to stock up her pantry and freezer in case the snow continued through the week.

Amanda guided the cart through the aisles and selected a variety of soup ingredients, more teas, and plenty of Sumatra coffee. Because of Indonesia's rare variety of tropics and regions, it is a perfectly structured environment for growing and producing her favorite coffees. She liked learning about the products she purchased. She loved that most of the Indonesian farms were small and family owned. Amanda checked all labels to be sure her coffee was fair trade and organic. She gave the brand bonus points whenever the label had a photo of the coffee's farmer.

By the time she completed her trip down the coffee aisle, she had loaded up several bags of the aromatic beans, more than usual. She couldn't bear the thought of running out of her morning brew if there was a blizzard. She was also fascinated with the interesting stories and farming information on the bags. She was the exact consumer the brilliant marketers had in mind while designing those bags of earthy beans.

Standing in front of the Ben & Jerry's row of

sweet concoctions, Amanda was visualized scoops of the frozen delights dolloped atop coffee and hot chocolate. She piled pints in her cart, including Mudslide, of course. She selected a variety of others: Chip Happens, Boots on the Moooo'n, and Chocolate Peanut Butter Split, which she thought would be perfect on hot chocolate. She had never met the creators of her adored ice cream, but she appreciated those entrepreneurs from Burlington, Vermont and was most certainly one of their biggest fans.

After Amanda had learned about the company's activist beliefs, she would never purchase another brand, considering the entrepreneurs heroes with a flair for delectable perfection.

"Thank you, Ben & Jerry," she said to herself.

Heading for the checkout line, Amanda realized more patrons had arrived. The store was getting crowded. She glanced through the front of the store and saw the snow coming down in huge chunks She was pleased her car would be waiting within a few steps from the front door.

Hurried, Amanda turned toward the shortest line when the wheel of her cart became stuck. With a little shove, she managed to get it moving again. A moment later only two out of the four wheels were functioning. Irritated, she gave the cart another push. and it unexpectedly flew out of her control. She lurched forward to grab hold of it but was seconds late. The cart crashed into a display of candy bars, many of the bars landing in her cart, but also all over the floor.

"Oh shit!" she blurted, instantly regretting speaking the thought aloud in a family environment. Now I'm causing a scene, she thought.

Exasperated and embarrassed, Amanda frantically started cleaning up the mess. Bending over to grasp the bars from the floor, she bumped heads with a stranger. He had also reached down to retrieve the bars in a kind gesture to help, but apparently misjudged how close they were to one another.

Amanda peered into the chocolate brown eyes of handsome dark-skinned man who had a pile of candy in his hands. She looked up at his well-worn, leather cowboy hat, wet from snow. Simultaneously, he looked down at her alpaca wool rainbow hat with earflaps.

"Interesting hat," they spoke perfectly in sync.

Smiling, neither said anything. They continued to work together and got the candy wreckage under control. She felt grateful but was also mortified. Amanda was suddenly burning hot in the wool hat and could feel her cheeks flushing like a teenager.

They stood in awkward silence for what felt like an eternity. All Amanda could manage was a sincere, feeble "Thanks." She hoped he could detect her gratitude. He tipped his hat in a polite gesture with a small smile and disappeared.

Amanda managed to calm down. She paid her bill and exited the store without incident. It was still snowing, but not as hard now. She lifted her face up to the cloudy sky and let the soft wet flakes touch her flushed face. The coolness was a relief. Hot flashes were a thing of the past, but those embarrassing moments in the store had the exact same feel.

She secretly wished the anonymous man would show up by her car, but she loaded her groceries alone. She glanced in the rearview mirror. She saw the beloved hat and scarlet cheeks which made her smile with a childlike grin that created a reminder of who she was. She was a real woman. She was sometimes clumsy. She was goofy. She was a lover of Ben & Jerry's ice cream, even in the winter. More relaxed, Amanda started her car.

The drive home did not include Bob Marley. She instead drove in silence, taking extra care not to get involved in any more accidents. She'd had enough for one day. She admired the beauty of the pristine snow and was looking forward to a quiet day at home.

When she arrived home and entered her kitchen, she threw some ingredients in her crockpot for a savory soup. A blazing fire and a nap were in her immediate future. How could one trip to the grocery store evoke such strong emotions and exhaustion? She had no idea.

The fire was roaring, and she'd stashed the groceries when she noticed a text message. Pulling her weighted blanket up over her body, she read the message.

"Hey Miss Mandy, I have a great idea for a dating site. Call me!"

Half-interested, but too tired to respond, Amanda decided to wait until later to call her back. Tomorrow maybe. Or next week. She wasn't sure when she'd ever be truly ready, but she did know her sweet neighbor would always have her best interest at heart.

Amanda napped long and hard. A wide brimmed cowboy hat, a silent blizzard, and the friendly oak tree sparkling with icicles in her backyard were present in a bizarre dream that she couldn't quite remember when she finally woke up.

When Amanda awoke, the aromatic soup in the crock pot bubbled and beckoned her to the kitchen. Savory chicken and rice soup with basil and sage from the summer garden was just what she needed on this cold day. She slathered a generous portion of Irish butter on the fresh crusty bread from the morning's embarrassing trip to the store. The nourishment rejuvenated her.

Amanda considered the text message from Casey and typed a quick reply with a sincere effort to sound upbeat.

"I'd love to hear the details."

She wasn't sure she actually planned to pursue this new opportunity.

Casey's response was immediate. "Check your email, I sent a list of questions for you to think about! I'll drop by sometime tomorrow, this is gonna be SO much fun."

Casey seemed to have enough enthusiasm for the two of them, which warmed Amanda's heart. "The younger generation must always be holding their phones, she noticed. They answer texts so fast."

Popcorn

Amanda was in a sassy, quirky mood; the sole life of the party in her cozy cottage on a winter day. She added Ben & Jerry's to her morning brew and was uncharacteristically considering a second cup as she moved toward the kitchen. Typically, one cup of the Sumatra blend had enough caffeine to fuel Amanda for the whole day. She felt frisky as she filled her favorite mug with the sunflower on the side for a second time.

Sitting in front of her laptop, she set out to complete the list of online dating profile questions from Casey. This was not a serious endeavor, yet she remained honest in her answers. Her strange, sarcastic side began to emerge in full force. Amanda threw caution to the wind with her answers, owning those that may be called eccentric.

Childhood memory: *mercurochrome and time*

out

Career aspirations as a child: *a mermaid or a chicken whisperer*

What do you miss about childhood: *underwear embroidered with the names of the week*

Your favorite food: *mustard makes me happy, Irish butter comes in a close second*

What are your fears? *mercury retrograde and marshmallows*

What is your favorite color? *lightning blue and rainbows*

Favorite type of social gathering: *if it involves fake smiling, I'm not going*

Describe your best friend: *a backyard hardwood, who is an oak tree, named Willie*

Hobbies: *puddle jumping with rubber rain boots, eating Ben & Jerry's ice cream, and naps*

Annoyances: *the random hairs that often grow on my chin and upper lip*

Clothing style: *tie dye*

Where do you see yourself in five years: *on a farm, preferably dancing with baby goats*

Describe yourself in a single sentence: *I'm an infinite, radiant beam of light made of stardust and sunshine with a hint of hurricane.*

Say a little about a good relationship: *I prefer to spend time with someone that faking my own death is not a consideration while we're together.*

Pet Peeve: *when an online form asks if I'm a robot; the hunk of metal they call a computer is a closer resemblance, and if you don't agree we can't be friends*

Favorite Song: *"If the Phone Doesn't Ring, It's Me"* by *Jimmy Buffet*

Casey showed up, as enthusiastic as ever. They hung out and crunched on buttered popcorn in front of the fire. "That little bluebird painting is adorable, Miss Mandy. It feels like he's got something to say." Casey remarked.

Amanda was pleased with Casey's compliment. "Thanks. I feel like he does talk to me!" The painting was professionally framed as a reward to herself for taking the project all the way to the end. The bluebird now hung proudly over the mantel.

"You sure have a lot of stuff in this room. There's barely room to walk around. Look at the piles of books, it's like a library in here. I love your crystals." Casey was talking aloud as she glanced around Amanda's living room. There was no judgment, just observations.

After the remarks regarding her surroundings, Amanda saw her young friend relax. They were ready to dig into Amanda's dating profile answers, which was the intention of her visit.

"I can't wait to read what you wrote. I hope you included that you're an artist, and that you used to be a teacher. This is awesome that you're letting me help you. I'm feeling honored that you don't still think of me as your annoying little neighbor anymore."

As Casey began read, there was a puzzled look

on her pretty face. Her full eyebrows were arched as her eyes widened. She attempted to remain valiantly supportive and open-minded. “Interesting,” she murmured. Casey grabbed a handful of buttered popcorn and munched. Finally, Casey blurted, “Miss Mandy, your answers are wacky!” There were a few times she opened her mouth to say more, but nothing came out of those beautiful lips, just more crunching. The intuitive young woman remained speechless for a few minutes as she read the remainder of the profile.

“Okay, I get the hint. You’re just not into this. You don’t need a dating profile, Miss Mandy.” They looked at one another, eyes smiling. “The perfect companion for you, if you’re to meet, is just going to show up. It will feel like a miracle. Like divine intervention. I want to be the first to meet him! Do we have a deal?”

“Of course, Casey, I’ll keep you up to date if anything interesting happens,” Amanda promised.

After Casey left, Amanda sat in her quiet cottage with Dalilah Belle snuggled at her feet. She looked at the walls, the floor, the ceiling. The fireplace, small embers keeping the room comfortable.

This place, my home, knows my story. This building is more than wood, nails, and decorative textiles. This building has observed my life. There have been joys and sorrows. This place has been here for me. This cottage that I’ve called home for decades is my sanctuary. A place for me to be still, but not to grow. There are limitations for me here.

I'm safe and secure. Yet growth and change will not occur here; it isn't meant to.

When Amanda came to this profound conclusion, she had no idea what was to come next. She sat quietly and ate the buttered popcorn thoughtfully.

She looked around her cottage and saw it through the eyes of transition, of change. "Nothing will change if I don't make it happen," she said aloud. Divine intervention is what Casey had called it. A miracle. Amanda believed in miracles. She also believed she herself was a miracle and was fully capable of creating change.

The days that followed were filled with serious decluttering work. She gathered and organized years of accumulations. Books that would not be read again, memorabilia she had collected on trips, gifts she felt obligated to store, some never used and covered in dust, items whose origins she did not recall. She packed up and donated clothing from her days of teaching along with all kinds of household items. She said goodbye to it all.

When she had sat on the couch that day following Casey's visit, savoring the last of the popcorn, the cottage had been unveiled so she could see her truth. She was literally surrounded by her past. It was revealed to her: "There is no room here for your future."

From that moment forward, she was felt divinely guided to transform her life, beginning with her home. Amanda recognized the abundance she eternally held in her heart, which was unrelated to what was in her cottage.

She filled her porch with donations and garbage cans over the following weeks. The more she removed, the lighter she felt. She was on a serious and valuable mission. Joyful and busy, Amanda noticed she felt youthful. An unfamiliar but welcomed burst of energy gave her the push to keep going. Pete, the post office worker, expressed his surprise at her progress and offered helpful ideas of how to donate items so they would be utilized in the best possible way. Catherine took teaching items and children's books to her grandchildren. "I always say, start them young. I hope the girls can foster a love for reading like I did when I was young. The twins are already showing signs of being gifted," Catherine boasted as she filled her car.

Amanda's neighbor, Al, showed up one afternoon, "Looks like you could use a hand." With his help they had managed to get some large pieces of furniture onto the porch. "Are you moving?" Al inquired.

Amanda responded vaguely, "Yes. Probably eventually."

Casey dropped by with news of a new apartment. With the help of a few strong friends and a truck, Casey carted off furniture, lamps, and household goods to fill her new place. Amanda was thrilled with the idea of this young friend creating a new home with some of her treasured belongings. It felt exactly right. It felt better than right. It was an honor to share her items with this kindred spirit.

Amanda sent her loving energy and good wishes along with the items for Casey's new beginning.

Amanda felt like a workhorse during the day. She gave no mercy to tangible items she had saved for years. At night, her thoughts were bathed in the possibility of romance and love. As she decluttered, and in some cases emptied, each room in her precious cottage, she saw glimpses of her future. She was ready to embrace the blessings coming her way.

Lynyrd Skynyrd's "Free Bird" blared on the stereo.

It was the beginning of an end for Amanda. A time of profound change. There was a magical transformation in her future, a result of her commitment. There were many unknowns, of course. But Amanda was ready for a new beginning, even without knowing the mysterious details. She trusted the universe to show her the way.

Bluebird House

Tony and Amanda sat on the swing and let the soft breeze rock them gently. They sat close with their hips, shoulders, and hands touching. Tony's cowboy hat was perched on his head, as always. They shared the occasional chat and a quick story amid hours of comfortable silence.

This is how it had been since Amanda moved into the farmhouse. As promised, Casey was her first visitor. She reported her apartment was shaping up nicely, mostly because of the furnishings lovingly provided by Amanda.

"Now, I need crystals," Casey mentioned in a serious tone. "After arranging my apartment, I realized that special vibe I always experienced in your cottage, and now here in the farmhouse, was a result of your collection. I don't completely understand the superpowers crystals hold, but I want some of it! Can you help me with good choices, Miss Mandy?"

Amanda knew of the magic in the bold selenite logs, sparkly gems tucked in corners and placed strategically around her space. I know some think they're merely decorations, she thought. But she trusted that they amplified happiness and protection, offering far more than their natural beauty.

Casey's request warmed Amanda's heart: crystals were her dear friends. The oldest object ever found on the planet was a four-billion-year old fragment of zircon. It was found somewhere in Australia. Amanda kept aware of the antiquity of crystals especially as she herself matured. She understood that age came with depth, and even hardship. Amanda took Casey's request seriously and provided the intuitive young woman with plenty of guidance. "Keep selenite on all of your windowsills. It's a crystal of purification." Amanda suggested. "And, if you need a boost for communication, blue lace agate will always be helpful," she added.

Amanda wore her familiar worn-out overalls on the farm where she was accepted and welcomed in a warm and wonderful way. She had grown accustomed to helping with the cows and chickens. Her herb garden flourished like never before, and everything felt as if this were exactly where she belonged.

Bryan, the owner and chef at the cafe, came by on a weekly basis. Amanda provided large bundles of her fresh herbs. Since the discovery of Amanda's ample garden, Bryan started to change up the menu frequently, utilizing the bountiful and aromatic harvest from the fields. He carted off bundles of rosemary, parsley, basil, and lemon balm.

Later in the week, Amanda and Tony sat at their table by the fireplace at Bryan's café, where they'd gone on their first date. They became regulars and always looked forward to seeing what Bryan would do with the harvest from their diligent work.

Amanda was impressed with the fact that Tony did not require an explanation about the value of harnessing the power of dirt. It was medicinal. He had a keen understanding related to the wondrous properties of soil under his fingernails. She loved that about him.

It had been an exciting time at the farm, due to the new additions. Spring was a happy time when babies are born. Baby goats were her favorite. She loved how they romped and raced. Their dancing and hilarious antics kept her laughing. She contemplated names for the newest kids, her head resting on Tony's shoulder:

Party Marty, Kick'n Kevin, Stinky Stella, and Happy Henry. Silliness, hilarity, and old-fashioned fun were what her life had been missing. Now she had laughter every day.

Dalilah Belle behaved like a rambunctious puppy. She wasn't used to so much land to roam around aimlessly. She adored her newly discovered animal friends. Her vigor and playful disposition fit perfectly at their farmhouse home.

Amanda and Tony cuddled close to one another on the porch swing, so content. It felt natural and easy. Tony draped his strong arms around her petite shoulders as the temperature began to drop. The swing was situated for a perfect view of the sunset. They liked their time on the porch to include the divine masterpiece, often feeling as if the colorful display was created for them alone.

After the magnificent sunset, they headed into their comfortable home. It had been another perfect, productive day. After a simple meal, prepared side by side in the old-fashioned, but well-equipped kitchen, they enjoyed dessert. The day Amanda had her few belongings delivered, Tony presented her with a surprise welcome gift. He had organized an entire freezer containing nothing but Ben & Jerry's ice cream!

He laughed, referring to that fortuitous day of fated introduction at the grocery store, "How could I not notice that you had the entire freezer section of Ben & Jerry's in your cart? And, that hat! Those crooked earflaps were hilarious. I knew if I laughed, you might take it the wrong way, though. I think I fell in love with you on that day. I couldn't stop thinking about you."

"I was hoping you'd be out by my car after I paid for the groceries. Of course, I had no idea what I would've said to you," she admitted. The surprise ice cream gift spoke volumes to Amanda. It was now their evening ritual: a shared bowl of well-crafted ice cream, always a sweet ending to every remarkable day together.

Nearby stood the new sturdy oak pole that held a beautifully handcrafted bluebird house. She felt Oliver nearby, as she always had. He approved of this new arrangement, she was sure of it.

Words of wisdom and hypnotic adventures with Willie were no longer necessary. Amanda held onto those experiences in her subconscious mind with gratitude. Now they communicated in new ways.

This was her Utopia: all of them living in perfect harmony.

Amanda occasionally heard whispers in the breeze and murmurs of love. She needn't comprehend the exact words. Sometimes there were familiar scents in the air that were reminiscent of her lively past.

Once, the bluebird landed directly on her knee. Theirs was an energetic connection. An unspoken communication that took her breath away. She often sat in solitude by the bluebird house. She understood that she wasn't really alone. Eyes closed, she experienced the gentle harmony of her past, present, and future.

For years they lived in solidarity, love, and continuous companionship, for which she was eternally grateful.

Tony understood completely, as she knew he would.

Additional Resources

Shrimp Salad

Chef Bryan Patrick

Ingredients:

1/2 cup creme fraiche (sour cream)

1 tablespoon olive oil

2 tablespoons fresh chopped dill

Zest of two lemons (or one tablespoon of minced preserved lemon rind)

Juice of one lemon

1 tablespoon Dijon

2 tablespoons shallots, minced

1 stalk celery, chopped

Salt and pepper to taste

1 pound cooked and deveined shrimp

Instructions:

Fold the dressing gently and bathe the shrimp with care.

Chill and serve with a wedge of lemon and a sprig of fresh parsley.

Cinnamon Rolls

Chef Colette Lynn

DOUGH AND FILLING
1 qt. whole milk
1 c. vegetable oil
1 c. sugar
2 packages active dry yeast (0.25 ounce packets)
8 c. (plus 1 cup extra, reserved) all-purpose flour
1 tsp. (heaping) baking powder
1 tsp. (scant) baking soda
1 tbsp. (heaping) salt
Plenty of melted butter
2 c. sugar
Generous sprinkling of cinnamon

FROSTING
1 bag powdered sugar
2 tsp. Nutmeg
1/2 c. milk
1/4 c. melted butter
1/4 c. brewed coffee
1/8 tsp. salt

Instructions:

For the dough: Heat the milk, vegetable oil, and sugar in a medium saucepan over medium heat to just below a boil. Set aside and cool to warm. Sprinkle the yeast on top and let it sit on the milk for 1 minute.

Add 8 cups of the flour. Stir until just combined, then cover with a clean kitchen towel, and set aside in a relatively warm place for 1 hour. After 1 hour, remove the towel and add the baking powder, baking soda, salt, and the remaining 1 cup flour. Stir thoroughly to combine.

Use the dough right away, or place in a mixing bowl and refrigerate for up to 3 days, punching down the dough if it rises to the top of the bowl. (Note: The dough is easier to work with if it has been chilled for at least an hour or so beforehand.)

To assemble the rolls, remove half the dough from the pan/bowl. On a floured baking surface, roll the dough into a large rectangle, about 30 x 10 inches. The dough should be rolled very thin.
To make the filling, pour 3/4 cup to 1 cup of melted butter over the surface of the dough. Use your fingers to spread the butter evenly. Generously sprinkle half of the ground cinnamon and 1 cup of the sugar over the butter. Don't be afraid to drizzle on more butter or more sugar! Gooey is the goal.

Now, beginning at the end farthest from you, roll the rectangle tightly towards you. Use both hands and work slowly, being careful to keep the roll tight. Don't worry if the filling oozes as you work; that just means the rolls are going to be divine. When you reach the end, pinch the seam together and flip the roll so that the seam is face down. When you're finished, you'll wind up with one long buttery, cinnamony, sugary, gooey log.

Slip a cutting board underneath the roll and with a sharp knife, make 1/2-inch slices. One "log "will produce 20 to 25 rolls. Pour a couple of teaspoons of melted butter into disposable foil cake pans (or regular 9-inch round cake pans) and swirl to coat. Place the sliced rolls in the pans, being careful not to overcrowd. (Each pan will hold 7 to 9 rolls.)

Repeat the rolling/sugar/butter process with the other half of the dough and more pans. Preheat the oven to 375°. Cover all the pans with a kitchen towel and set aside to rise on the countertop for at least 20 minutes before baking. Remove the towel and bake for 15 to 18 minutes, until golden brown. Don't allow the rolls to become overly brown.

While the rolls are baking, make the maple icing: In a large bowl, whisk together the powdered sugar, milk, butter, coffee, and salt. Splash in the maple flavoring. Whisk until very smooth.

Taste and add in more maple, sugar, butter, or other ingredients as needed until the icing reaches the desired consistency.

The icing should be somewhat thick but still very pourable.

Remove the pans from the oven. Immediately drizzle icing over the top. Be sure to get it all around the edges and over the top. As they sit, the rolls will absorb some of the icing's moisture and flavor.

They only get better with time... not that they last for more than a few seconds.

The Joy of Crystals in Your Home

Rose Quartz (shades of pink, mauve, and light lavender)

Place a few near doorways, especially the entrance of your home to bring peace, love, and harmony to all who enter. Keep a small bowl of these crystals to share with others whenever it feels appropriate. Everyone needs rose quartz!

Blue Lace Agate (light blue, often looks layered)

Use this gemstone in a place where communication takes place, such as near a laptop or where you may frequently use your phone. Also, tuck one in your purse or bra if going on a job interview or facing any situation where speaking your truth is appropriate.

Amethyst (many shades of purple, rare ones are green)

Consider this purple beauty for calmness. It's a lovely crystal to promote wonderful sleep. It is also known to support the ability to accept yourself more fully. Place anywhere in the home, especially near your nighttime pillow for deep, restorative rest.

Malachite (dark green, sometimes with embedded spheres of light green)

This crystal promotes positive changes in life. Use when meditating on a new direction in life or amping up some of your current situations. Your awareness will be expanded when using this crystal. Do not get this crystal wet or use it near food.

Selenite (opaque white)

This amazing crystal is used for cleansing, protection, and purifying. Place on the windowsills of every room. Any crystal paired with a selenite will be purified, too. This crystal should not be wet, it will melt.

Hold crystals in the palms of your hands with your eyes closed. Ask the crystal if it wants to be a part of your home. Openly set the intentions with your crystals when you decide to invite them into your home. Feel, know, and trust your intuition. Some crystals will bring forth tears. Stored emotions can be released, so don't avoid crying. There is a gem to be found within every teardrop.

Let your crystals be your friends, your advocates, and know that sometimes you may decide to share them with others. They aren't always meant to stay with us forever.

Sneak Peek

Sophie was standing next to her mailbox when the new neighbor approached.

“I’m Amanda, from around the corner," she announced, as if Sophie had been expecting her.

“It looks like you could use this,” the petite lady said.

Reaching into the pocket of her ripped jeans, Amanda withdrew and presented Sophie a glowing rose quartz.

“My name is Sophie. Oh my, thanks. It’s beautiful.”

Sophie accepted the unexpected gesture of kindness. She was astounded by the perfection of this crystal, representing love. She knew all about rose quartz and the ability to mend a broken heart.

This brief encounter was the beginning of a friendship that neither had realized they needed.
Amanda lifted Sophie’s spirits on the exact day when she was in desperate need of that rose quartz. Amanda had placed the rock in her pocket before she set out for her walk.

“I feel like this sweet gem is going to be re-homed today,” was her only thought.

Divinely guided many times in the past, Amanda had learned to simply comply when she felt her intuition inspire her.

“How did she know about the conflict I endure each year on this day?” Sophie wondered.

It was an anniversary for Sophie that only a few knew about.

Sophie had lost her only child that same day two decades ago.

The number of trips around the sun made no difference. The date on the calendar hit her like a punch in the gut each year.

She had been moping around under a dark cloud of anger and despair when Amanda strolled past.

Sophie occupied the single log cabin in her community, it was nestled among a variety of farmhouses. From the outside, the cabin looked old fashioned and cozy.

For those who were lucky enough to enter Sophie's home, there were always gasps of' "Oh, what a surprise!"

The interior of the modest log cabin was filled with carvings, statues and artifacts from all over the world. Sophie had been a world traveler from a young age.

She was now settled into a quieter life, surrounded by relics and artwork from every corner of the globe. Her home was a true showpiece, and for visitors it was like entering a world class museum. Sophie had a knack of arranging the contents of her home which would far exceed the price of the log cabin. For this reason, Sophie had a state-of-the-art alarm system installed when she had moved to the small community a few years ago.

Sophie sat quietly that evening, holding the special rose quartz crystal in her hand.

"I already know Amanda and I will become close friends. I felt her warmth the moment she walked up to my mailbox this morning." Her thoughts were optimistic.

She added the crystal to a silver bowl that sat on the table next to the well-worn blue velvet loveseat. The bowl contained selenite hearts, several citrine gemstones, a deep orange aragonite and a variety of natural agates. Selenite was one of Sophie's favorites - pure white gems that provided a sense of purity and cleansing. The gleaming pink of the rose quartz added a beautiful touch to her collection.

"Is it possible the neighbor, Amanda, had the ability to look straight into my heart?" Sophie wondered.

Sophie stirred sweet local honey into her tea mug. It was a calming ritual she had developed as she readied herself for bed each evening. Her favorite brand of tea offered messages, which often brought her insight and it was fun to read the notes. The tea bag message tonight read, "Culinary delights create relationships that are everlasting."

As Sophie rested in bed, she was thinking about culinary delights while making a grocery list in her head. She had sampled food from so many corners of the earth and had learned to recreate many of the dishes.

The Mediterranean foods from the Greek Island, Santorini would always be her favorites. The foods included stuffed grape leaves, figs and aromatic moussaka. Coming in a close second would be the cuisine from West Africa, especially the fragrant fish soup made with sweet fresh coconut. Cooking was therapeutic for Sophie. Sharing her creative and diverse dishes always brought deep satisfaction.

Right before drifting off to sleep, Sophie decided, "I'm going to invite Amanda over for lunch sometime soon."

Made in the USA
Middletown, DE
08 June 2021